FIFTY YEARS LATER

JAMES J. COLLINS

ISBN: 0692979441
ISBN-13:9780692979440

For my wife
Rebecca A. McDiarmid

Acknowledgments

The author is grateful for the suggestions and critical review of early drafts of this story by Linda Cross, Linda Thomas, and other members of the Cape Fear Fiction Writers group. Jason Frye of Teakettle Junction Productions improved the book with his substantive and editorial reviews.

Other sources that supported the book's creation are listed below in the Resources section.

Government efforts in the 1960s and 1970s to construct a dam at Tocks Island in the Delaware Water Gap area of Pennsylvania are used to frame the story told herein, but the book is a work of fiction. All events and characters are products of the author's imagination and are used fictitiously.

Resources

Albert, Richard C. *Damning the Delaware: The Rise and Fall of the Tocks Island Dam.* The Pennsylvania State University, 1987.

Bob Dylan Lyrics: 1962–2001. New York, Simon and Schuster, 2004.

East Stroudsburg State University, Kemp Library.

Monroe County Historical Society, Stroudsburg, Pennsylvania.

Monroe County Public Library, Stroudsburg, Pennsylvania.

New York Times Online Archive: 1851–1980.

Pocono Record Archives, 1970–1974.

Saved from the Dam. Cultural Resource Management, National Park Service, v. 2, no. 3, 2002.

There's a battle outside and it's ragin'
It'll soon shake your windows and rattle your walls
For the times they are a changin'

Bob Dylan
The Times They Are A-Changin' (1963)

Author's Note

In northeastern Pennsylvania, the Delaware River wore a gap through the Pocono Mountains over millions of years. Soil and stone gave way, and the river cut into the bedrock, creating the Delaware Water Gap. The Poconos, part of the Appalachian mountain chain, form a lush valley with the Delaware River meandering through. Viewed from the river a few miles north, the vista inspires awe.

Historically the area was called the Minisink Valley or simply the Minisink. The name derives from the Lenape Indians, the First Nations people who inhabited the valley before the Europeans arrived. Some old-timers still use the name, but before long it will likely go out of common use.

During the first fifty or sixty years of the twentieth century, the Minisink was a popular tourist destination for the urban populations of New York City and Philadelphia. In the 1950s and 1960s, a small population of commuters to New York City and northern New Jersey made permanent homes there, adding to the population. The newcomers adopted the laid-back lifestyle of the area, so it absorbed them and retained its rustic flavor. The small cities of Stroudsburg and East Stroudsburg in the valley provided urban conveniences.

In 1962, the federal government enacted legislation to build a dam across the Delaware River several miles above the Delaware Water Gap. The Tocks Island Dam Project required land, and lots of it; people were forced to sell farms and homesteads they had occupied for generations. In the end, fifteen thousand people were displaced, three thousand to five thousand dwellings and outbuildings were demolished, and hundreds of historical sites were destroyed. The razed land sat vacant for years.

Outsiders came to squat on the empty land. Their hippie lifestyle contrasted sharply with that of the residents and became a source of conflict. As the disruptive aspects of dam-building operations ground on, opposition to the dam grew. Then the country's nascent environmental movement began focusing on Tocks Island Dam's adverse impacts on the watershed, the animals, and the plants. The dam was never built, but the struggle between pro- and antidam forces dragged on for more than a decade.

In many ways, the Tocks Island Dam–controversy mirrored conflict in the country writ large. Unrest was endemic. Race riots, assassinations, the civil-rights movement, campus unrest, and opposition to the Vietnam War roiled the country between the mid-1960s and mid-1970s. Toward the end of the period, Watergate added turmoil and conflict.

Now, in the first two decades of the twenty-first century, the area retains its natural beauty, thanks to the creation of the Delaware Water Gap National Recreation Area, a seventy-thousand-acre park. But the creation of this natural asset has a dark history: it grew out of the failed effort to build a dam a half century ago.

This novel explores how the attempt to build a dam in the Delaware Water Gap National Recreation Area impacted the local people and their community. Though the story is told through a group of fictional characters created by the author, their actions and reactions, the things they say, and the lives they lead demonstrate the human costs tied to the dam.

Sam Kopco

As I eased my new canoe into the Delaware River, I wondered how much longer I would be able to take this trip. I hopped into the aft seat as the canoe drifted away from the bank. Two strokes pushed me out into the quiet current flowing south. The sun was still below the trees in the east, so the night sky lingered, the moon low and waxing, just past full. Still, the earliest of song-birds were calling to each other.

I was alone on the river—just the way I like it. The water looked black, but I knew it was brown, muddied from the recent rain. The Delaware Water Gap, seven miles ahead, was still covered in mist; it will clear before I leave the river.

I was satisfied to move at the speed of the current, so I used my paddle only to keep me pointed south. The northern point of Tocks Island came into view as I rounded a bend. It was dense with tree cover—all hardwoods best I could tell. I camped there as a boy in the mid-1950s when it was called Worthington Island. The island was less than a mile long and only about 150 yards at its

1

widest point. I decided to look. The island would disappear under a huge lake if the Tocks Island Dam was built.

I dug two hard strokes to push the bow of my canoe onto the shoreline, pulled the canoe further up, and walked through the thick weeds into the woods. When I got inside the tree line, the birds quieted. I turned to look for the two old cabins that were built here decades ago. The Worthington family built them and then abandoned them as their children grew up and lost interest in the outdoors.

When I was a boy, my grandfather and I used to sleep in our sleeping bags on the floor in one of the cabins, but by now, though, the cabins had been abandoned for years. The roof had collapsed into one of them, floorboards broke through under foot, and trees grew through the porches.

I followed the former footpath, still faintly visible, and walked carefully to avoid twisting my ankle on the tree roots and fist-size stones that hid under the weeds. The birds restarted their chatter.

In a few minutes, I saw the hulk of the first cabin. Grandpop Pete and I stayed in the second one, but when I got to it, I found that the short staircase up into it was rotted and unsafe, the entrance too high to reach. I realized it would be crumbling inside anyway, and before long, the Tocks Island Dam lake would obliterate it.

I recalled the smell of the cabin. The odor inside was no different from outside. Grandpop would be asleep and snoring softly only minutes after we turned the lantern off, but I did not sleep quickly. I worried about mice and snakes—afraid they would crawl across my face or, worse, that they might creep into my sleeping bag. Eventually, though, the sounds of the crickets settled me. I'd listen for the hoot of an owl but would usually fall asleep before I heard one.

Back in my canoe, I continued down the river to the Water Gap, digging my paddle deep for the last mile. I was sweating and breathing heavily when I pulled my canoe onto the shoreline.

I decided to reward myself with a beer and headed to the Village Tavern in Stroudsburg. It had just opened for the day. Emil, the owner and daytime bartender, was preparing for the day's customers, and I was the first. A rack of beer mugs from the dishwasher sat on top of the bar behind the beer tap. The Rolling Stones played loudly on the jukebox. Soundless images flickered on the TV high on the wall behind the bar. Emil reached under the bar and turned the jukebox volume down.

"I smell trouble. Sam Kopco's gettin' an early start."

"Shut up and give me a draft," I said.

"Oh my, your hemorrhoids bothering you?"

"Just thirsty, M. Just thirsty."

Emil drew a beer, sloughed off the excess froth, and set it on a coaster in front of me.

Located in the middle of the block on Main Street in downtown Stroudsburg, the Village Tavern had a dingy look from the sidewalk, as if it was closed or half-closed or would close any day now. Heavy curtains covered the only windows in the place, and the ones in the front needed washing; the ones in the back were still more whole than broken, but that was some minor miracle. For a place that was only fifty years old, it felt older, like a permanent part of the town. The place had the feel of midnight all the time. But Emil kept things spotless. He scrubbed the bar and equipment so that it all shone. After closing, someone came in each night to scrub the floor and clean the men's and women's bathrooms, although female customers were few, usually only seen on Saturday night. Emil was finicky about keeping a clean place. He blamed it on his German heritage.

The room was long and narrow—the mahogany bar occupied forty feet along the right wall, and five booths lined the left wall. A rear section had a shuffleboard table and dartboard. The restrooms were at the back.

"What brings you in so early, Sam?"

"Just got off the river. Came down from above Tocks Island. Testing my new canoe; I really like it."

"No work today?" he asked, stopping his own.

"Needed a day off. Been working six days a week for a couple of months."

An anguished look on the man's face on the television screen caught my attention. His face was familiar, but I couldn't put a name to him. Speaking into the cameras, his distress was obvious. Words struggled from his mouth.

"M, turn the TV up!"

Emil reached up and turned the volume dial. The shaky voice spoke.

"Robert Francis Kennedy died at one forty-four a.m. today, June sixth, 1968. With Senator Kennedy at the time of his death were his wife, Ethel; his sisters, Mrs. Stephen Smith and Patricia; brother-in-law Stephen Smith, and Mrs. John F. Kennedy. He was forty-two years old..."

Emil and I looked at each other, stunned.

"Bobby's dead?" Emil sounded doubtful.

I was quiet—trying to get my head around what the man had said.

"This is fuckin' crazy!" Emil shouted. "What happened?"

"I don't know, but if you'll shut up, they'll tell us."

We listened as Frank Mankiewicz answered reporters' questions about Robert Kennedy's assassination—how he was shot in the head by Sirhan Sirhan, a Jordanian immigrant, in the kitchen of the Ambassador Hotel in Los Angeles just after winning the Democratic Presidential Primary Election in California. Surgery to save the New York Senator had been unsuccessful. His remains were being flown back east in the company of family members, including his wife, Ethel; his sister-in-law, Jacqueline Kennedy; and his sole surviving brother, Massachusetts Senator Edward Kennedy.

"The country's coming apart," Emil said. "First JFK, then King, now Bobby. I don't care for his politics—didn't like his politics, but I think his heart was in the right place. Vietnam, the race riots—even this Tocks Island Dam thing. We're in a mess."

"I would've voted for him," I said. "He's right on Vietnam. We need to be out of there."

"You were over there, Sam, so I respect your opinion, but with all the money and lives we've spent on that war, I hate to see us leave with our tail between our legs."

I didn't respond. Talking about the war made me nervous. When people found I'd been in combat over there, they wanted to know if I'd killed anyone, asked for details about the fighting in the jungle, or argued about whether we should be fighting over there at all. I didn't want to talk about any of it, especially those bloody months in the jungle.

I sipped my beer. "Anything going on I should know about?"

"Have you heard about Stan Lutz's wife?"

I put down my beer, curious as Stan Lutz's wife wasn't one to be mentioned in the bar gossip. "No, what happened?" I asked.

"Killed herself. Ran a hose from Stan's pickup exhaust into the cab and ended it."

"That's awful. When did that happen?"

"Early yesterday. Funeral's Friday."

"Her family had been on that land for generations."

"The Army Corps of Engineers stole that land. Didn't pay them half what it's worth," Emil answered.

"Yeah. The Lutzes are living in a rented house in town, while the hippies squat rent-free in their old house. It'd make me crazy."

Emil continued his preparations for the day's customers. A dozen mugs were neatly arranged on the right of the beer tap and a dozen shot glasses on the left.

The Village Tavern felt like a safe place for me, and its low light enhanced that effect. It was rarely crowded during the day; a small crowd came for a sandwich and a beer at lunch, and just after work, a bunch stopped for a drink. But it got crowded at night— especially Friday and Saturday nights. The customers were mostly men, but on weekend nights, a few wives or girlfriends came with their partners. Single women rarely came to the Village. I liked it better during the week.

The TV sound was off again, and I watched Bobby Kennedy making a silent speech on the screen. "How's Stan Lutz doing?"

"I haven't seen him, but I'll go to the wake."

"It's at Jankowski's, I guess."

"Right. Seven o'clock, Thursday."

I sat quietly sipping my beer and finally spoke, almost to myself: "There's gonna be trouble."

"Gonna be," said Emil. "You think it's gonna get worse?"

"I do. Folks are pissed. I'm pissed. The Corps is still forcing people off their land. Those hippie flower assholes squatting there just to insult us. At some point, a bunch of state and federal cops are going to come to kick their asses out if we don't do it first. I think it's going to blow up one of these days."

"You may be right. What worries me is that we'll get the worst of it all. They've already stolen a lot of our land, and it's just not peaceful around here anymore. I was afraid there was going to be trouble here the other night."

"Yeah?"

"A couple of those hippies came in, sat at the bar, and ordered beers. It got kinda quiet. I was busy, but the hair on the back of my neck tells when something's in the air. I started watchin' Tommy Farrell. You know how he gets after he's had a few. He was staring at one of them. Guy had long blond hair, kind of a patchy beard. He looked like he could take care of himself, but I knew Tommy was looking for an excuse to go after him. I worried it was going to get ugly."

"Nothing came of it?"

"No. I think the hippies sensed the hostility and left after one beer."

The morning rush-hour traffic outside was barely audible over the sound of the bar's refrigeration. Finally, I asked, "Do you think the dam's a good idea?"

7

"I think it could be good in the long run—for flood control, for the economy. But I hate the price we're paying. I think the turmoil is going to leave scars for a long time."

"You know what really pisses me off, M?"

"What?"

"It doesn't make a fuckin' bit of difference what we think. The folks in Washington and Harrisburg and Trenton and New York have decided we're going to get a dam, period. And they don't give a shit who gets hurt along the way."

"I am having second thoughts," Emil answered. "Till now, I've been thinking better flood control, cheaper electricity...and a big lake to boat and fish on would be nice—good for business. But I heard there's a new study saying the lake would die after a few years. Pollution and runoff from New York will wash down the river, kill the fish, and leave a thick green scum on the lake. If that's true, it's a deal breaker for me."

"The bad news keeps comin'," I said. I didn't want to discuss pros and cons.

After my second beer, I decided to go to my cabin for a nap.

When I left the Village, I went to the pay phone down the street and called Holly at work.

"Commissioners' office," Holly answered.

"I'm horny," I said, trying to sound sexy.

"Yes, sir. I have most of that information, but there are one or two things that I want to check. Can you call again in about an hour?"

"Do you think we can get together after work?"

"Probably. But I'll let you know when you call back."

"Good. I lust for you."

Holly worked in the Monroe County Commissioners' office and sometimes couldn't talk to me on the telephone. Her estranged husband's father, Leo Kober, was a county commissioner. So far, we'd been able to keep our affair secret. Holly's mother and her friend Claudia knew, but if her estranged husband, Mark, or his father had found out, she's convinced it would create problems with her divorce and job. I had to agree.

"I'll call again in an hour."

When I called back, Holly answered. "Commissioners' office."

"Can you talk?"

"Mark's father was standing beside my desk when you called earlier."

"I've been thinking about you."

"Mmm. That's nice. My mother can babysit Rachel for a few hours. I'll drop her off after work."

"Great. How about I pick you up at our regular place?"

"Yes. Six o'clock?"

"Fine. Want me to get some Chinese takeout?"

"How about pizza instead?"

"That's good."

I headed out of town to my cabin at the end of a gravel road just north of Shawnee. My closest neighbor was half a mile away.

When I was a boy, my grandfather and I hunted deer in the forest beyond the cabin. Those are happy memories. Grandpop Pete was a quiet, kind man, and I enjoyed hanging out with him. He let me do things most boys my age were not allowed to do. On my tenth birthday, he gave me an expensive Remington hunting rifle with a scope and taught me how to use and care for it.

During my time in Vietnam, and while I was recovering from my wounds, my army pay built up in the bank. I bought the cabin with two acres right after my discharge. It wasn't comfortable to live in year-round yet. No central heating, but I'd made some improvements. I liked its isolation, and its connection to my boyhood.

The cabin was about one thousand square feet. I'd insulated the roof and walls, upgraded the electrical and plumbing, and replaced the drafty windows. One of my high-school wrestling teammates, now a local contractor, was going to install central heating when I got the money together, but the costs of improving the cabin kept me broke, and I hadn't had a vacation for two years. Recently, I'd decided to take a break and make do with the woodstove for warmth. Central heat could wait.

When it got too cold or when I got tired of haulin' wood in for the stove, I stayed at my mom's. She was always glad when I came home and didn't give me a hard time about the way I lived. But I knew she worried about my need to stay isolated and me not being married. She didn't know about Holly, and I'd decided not to tell her, seein' that Holly wasn't divorced yet.

I came in the back door, unlaced my boots, left them on the floor just inside, and pulled off my hooded sweat shirt as I headed for the bedroom. Letting my Levi's drop, I fell into the unmade bed I'd left just a few hours ago and checked to make sure my handgun was in place between the sideboard and mattress, and, with the help of the beer, I was asleep in minutes.

My recurrent nightmare woke me. I always wake up at the same point in the dream: just as my pet monkey is killed.

Early in my time in the Vietnam jungle, I found a small monkey in the underbrush, apparently abandoned by its mother. I nursed the emaciated animal and watched it grow and then thrive. The little guy was gray with a pale underside, had black hands and feet, and a brownish-orange face. I named him Ace, and he became the platoon's mascot.

Ace was entertaining. He hopped from shoulder to shoulder, had a fondness for the chocolate in our meal kits, liked a lot of sugar in his black coffee, and smoked cigarettes without inhaling. Friendly to everyone in the platoon except the sergeant, he always slept with me and sat on my shoulder when we were on patrol.

One day when I was walking point through the jungle, Ace started to growl softly, and as I continued moving forward, his growls got louder. We stopped, but Ace hopped around growling. Then someone spotted a partially buried booby trap in the trail just in front of us. When Ace reacted like this on another occasion, we trained him to walk just ahead of the platoon as we moved through the jungle. He warned us a few times.

On one occasion, Ace spotted something. We stopped and disarmed it, but when we moved on again with Ace in front, a second device exploded, blowing Ace apart. We found only bits of him to bury.

Ace's death disabled the platoon for days. We refused to go on patrol and stopped talking to one another. There were a couple of fights. It wasn't only Ace's death—we'd had several casualties and had been out in the jungle too long without a break. We were worn out. In a few days, a full bird colonel from the command center visited us in the field and threatened courts-martial, so we went back to work. But it was scarier; Ace's vigilance had been reassuring.

During my ten months in the central Vietnam jungle, I saw a lot of blood, but it was Ace's death that haunted me. I didn't dream about the lost men or the ugly wounds. I always saw the flash of the explosion that killed Ace and a large patch of his gray fur stuck to a tree beside me. That's when I wake up.

I got out of bed, was tempted to have a beer, but instead grabbed a can of black-bean soup from my collection of canned goods, heated the contents on my two-burner gas stove, and brewed a pot of coffee. I sat facing the large window over the kitchen sink that looks out into the woods. A light wind rustled the leaves. The sun found openings through the mature hardwoods and dropped dappled bright spots on the ground.

I need some bright things on these walls, I thought. There were two pictures from 'Nam that my mom had framed on the wall. One shows most of my platoon in ragged fatigues in the middle of a clearing. I'm on the left end of the front row, arms folded across my chest, unsmiling. The other picture, taken the same day, shows me and my close buddy Kirk, who has his arm around my shoulders. Kirk is smiling. Again, I look unhappy. *Why am I so glum?* I wondered.

The pictures may prolong the war for me, but I can't take them down. It would violate the brotherhood. The only other picture on my walls showed me getting a second-place ribbon at the state high-school wrestling championships in my senior year—my dark-blue wrestling singlet revealing a wiry, strong body. I missed winning the state title in my weight class that year by one point in the final match. I wrestled at 160 pounds, occasionally at 170 when Coach asked me to "go up" a weight class, if it was likely to add to the team's total points.

I wondered what I might hang on the walls. Maybe a waterfall coming down a mountain. Or colorful hot-air balloons: I'd seen a large poster like this recently. Huge yellow, red, and blue multicolored balloons lifting off the ground somewhere, with mountains in the distance.

Spooning my soup, I recalled my dream about Ace. It worried me. At this point, more than two years after my discharge, I thought I'd be free of flashbacks. I had not had any reactions in public, but I feared it might happen. I can live with the dreams. But acting crazy in public would humiliate me. I worried especially that Holly would see me lose control.

I spent a lot of time at that cabin after the army. I was still weak physically. They left some shrapnel in my neck because it was too risky to remove, so it took a while to build my strength back. My head was another story, though. It was really messed up, and it took months to quiet it down. I slept a lot, drank beer, listened to music, and walked in the woods. I'd have four or five cases of beer delivered out there every week or so. I know my mother worried about me, but I had to be alone. I didn't trust myself around people.

For a long time after I came home, music and beer kept me from unraveling. Since I was a boy, I'd listened to music, and in the army, I learned about different kinds of music—found out I liked some country music and discovered Mississippi Delta Blues. I accumulated a bunch of seventy-eight records and still have some of them, even though I don't have a machine to play them on anymore. Back then, the music transported me to other places, and the beer dulled me.

Today when I hear those old songs that touched me then, I get tears in my eyes. Simon and Garfunkel's "Bridge Over Troubled

Waters" brought my grief to the surface and gave me hope at the same time. Don McLean's songs spoke to me. I liked some of Bob Dylan's and Leonard Cohen's music. James Brown and James Taylor stirred me in different ways. Recently I replaced Carole King's *Tapestry*, a 78 rpm album, from the early 1970s with a tape and occasionally listen to it now. So when I say beer and music rescued me, I mean it. The music helped connect me back to who I was before the war and, eventually, gave me the courage to look forward.

Before I went to meet Holly, I called my army buddy, Kirk. He lived in Pittsburgh, had his own construction business, and usually worked from 6:00 a.m. and knocked off in midafternoon. Kirk and I talked every couple of weeks. He was the only one I didn't have to explain things to—knew what I meant even if I didn't say it clear. He had his own Vietnam demons. He never got wounded like me, but he stayed on after I was evacuated when our platoon had more bloody times. Kirk was married and had two kids. He answered before the second ring.

"How're you doin', Kirk?"

"Sam! Good to hear from you. I'm doin' okay. How about you?"

"I'm doin' good—really. Just don't feel that way."

"Are you still workin'?"

"Yeah. Love the job. Especially this time of the year. I'm out in the woods most of the time. My boss leaves me alone. Just lets me do my job."

"Are you and Holly still together?"

"Yeah…well, we're still seeing each other. I'm going to pick her up in a little while. I don't see her that often, though, and we keep a low profile. Her divorce is goin' slow."

"Yeah, I can see that'd be frustrating. It's temporary, though, right?"

"I think so…hope so."

"I'll bet it works out."

"I had another dream about Ace," I said after a too-long pause.

"I'm sorry, Sam. I know that brings it all back."

"I wonder if it's ever going to go away!"

"My flashbacks still come too. The scary one for me is when that gook got within five feet of me in a firefight after you were evacuated. I still see his face. I fired in the nick of time."

"That's scary."

"It usually happens during the night for me. I'll sit up in bed. Heather tells me I holler first."

"Wakes her up too, huh?"

"Yeah. And I can't go right back to sleep. I have to get out of bed for a while."

"Do you drink then?"

"No. I've quit doin' that. When I started drinkin' in the middle of the night, it really scared Heather."

"I'm drinkin' a lot less too."

"Just makes it worse, don't it?"

"Yeah. But sometimes it's the only thing that chases the thoughts away."

"Well, aren't we a fuckin' mess?" Kirk said with a laugh.

"I hope no one is listening."

Kirk and I talked for a while. I felt better after I hung up, but I was concerned about Kirk. It sounded like he and Heather were having a rough time.

I was waiting when Holly pulled into the parking lot. I could feel the smile on my face even before she got out of her car. She was smiling too when she hopped into my pickup. She squeezed my face between her hands and kissed me hard.

"On my God," she said. "A friendly face; I feel like I'm surrounded by enemies at work."

"Shall I bring my gun into your office and take care of them?"

"I wish it were so simple, Sam. Take me away from here."

Holly moved closer to me as I waited for a break in traffic and turned out of the parking lot. It was only a six- or eight-minute drive to my cabin. I was aroused along the way. Just inside the cabin door, we enjoyed a long embrace and then went immediately to the bathroom, where I turned the shower on full hot.

Holly's white blouse buttoned down the front. I freed all six buttons, slipped it off, and reached behind to unhook her bra. I stopped undressing her while I kissed her breasts. She stepped out of her skirt and waited for me to remove her panties. I lowered the panties and paused here too while I knelt to kiss between her legs. I stood up and pulled my shirt over my head while she loosened my belt, unbuttoned my jeans, and laughed at the trouble she had lowering the zipper past my erection.

The small bathroom was filled with steam now. I adjusted the temperature, and we stepped under the water. I kept two bars of soap in the shower so we could soap each other at the same time. On this day, we had our first orgasms with the water pelting our bodies.

We dried each other in the warm bathroom and rushed through the cool air from the bathroom to the bedroom. Under the covers, we moved our still-moist bodies together. I dozed—I think it was only a few minutes—and opened my eyes to see Holly staring at me with a half smile in her eyes.

"You look like a boy when you sleep."

"I'm happy."

"Oh, so am I, Sam. So am I. I wish we could stay here forever."

But all we had that day was a couple of hours.

I was never comfortable in crowds, and it had gotten worse since Vietnam, but I decided to go to Vera Lutz's wake. I figured it was time to see whether I could stomach being in a crowd; plus, I wanted to be a witness with my neighbors. Most folks in the Valley thought the government was responsible for Mrs. Lutz's suicide, and I wanted them to know I was with them.

It was crowded at the funeral home, seemed like half the town was there. At first the crowd didn't bother me, but then it did. I felt their eyes on me, heard the buzz of their conversation like hornets swarming. My clothes didn't help either. I hadn't worn a coat and tie, since I don't remember when. Both my white shirts were too tight to button at the collar, and I realized my only necktie looked like something my grandfather would wear, and it may have been an old tie of his. My blazer was tight; I was afraid it might split down the back.

The line to go into Jankowski's Funeral Home was out the door and halfway down the sidewalk to the corner. I stood at the back of the line. There was a bunch of teenagers, boys and girls, right in front of me, and they were chattering like kids. They were dressed different from kids when I was their age. One tall boy wore these striped bell-bottom pants and a white shirt with a ruffle in the front. He looked like a joke to me. Two of the girls wore short skirts—

halfway up their thighs. They reminded me of the cheerleaders in high school. I'm pretty sure one well-endowed girl wasn't wearing a bra. She caught me lookin' at her, so I looked away.

I looked forward at the line and didn't recognize anybody. Right after I stood in line, an older couple got in line behind me. I didn't recognize them either. We moved ahead slowly, and more people lined up at the back.

After a few minutes, I felt a light tap on my shoulder. The man behind me asked, "You're Sam Kopco, aren't you?"

"Yes, sir."

I didn't recognize him. Dressed neatly in a dark suit with a fresh starched white shirt and a black necktie, he looked like a banker or a funeral director. But he seemed comfortable dressed like that.

"I knew your grandfather. We used to play cards at the VFW." He paused and smiled. "He used to take my money. He was a mean poker player." He hesitated again and spoke in a more serious tone. "Welcome home."

My throat closed, so I just nodded.

"I'm sorry," he said. "I'm Peter Marsh, and this is my wife, Emily. Terrible about Mrs. Lutz, isn't it?"

I was still off-balance and didn't know who Mrs. Lutz was, at first.

Peter Marsh saw my confusion and rescued me.

"I don't think Mrs. Lutz ever got over losing her land."

I got my voice back. "I know. Emil told me."

Now he looked confused. So I went on. "Emil, at the Village Tavern, told me about Mrs. Lutz."

"Oh, of course."

"I didn't know my grandfather was a poker player."

Peter Marsh laughed. "The best around here. Said he sharpened his skills in the navy in Second World War. Nothing else to do most of the time floating around the South Pacific on a ship."

Emily Marsh said, "I'll bet you're glad to be back home."

"Yes, ma'am."

"I just don't know what to think about that war halfway around the world."

"It is a long way off." I never figured out how to respond to comments about the war and often said something that seemed dumb when I thought about it later. Not sure what to say next, I turned away and looked ahead.

The line moved forward. There were still fifteen or twenty people in front of me before the door to the funeral home. I stood silently.

Finally, I entered the vestibule. The smell of fresh flowers made the air heavy and sweet, almost sickening. I couldn't yet see into the room with the casket. In ten minutes or so, I was standing on the threshold of the large room, looking directly across at a shiny black-and-gray casket that looked like it weighed a ton. I hoped they wouldn't ask me to be a pallbearer. I was relieved the lid was closed, but I wondered why. I'd only been to a couple of wakes, and the lid was open at them. In 'Nam, we tried to hide the damage to the bodies, but I didn't think Mrs. Lutz was mutilated, so I didn't understand the closed casket.

I noticed some familiar faces in the small clusters of people talking quietly. My Pocono Electric boss was across the room, and when I caught his eye, he waved. My high-school wrestling coach was sitting in a wingback chair along the wall. I couldn't get his attention.

19

There were still eight or ten people ahead of me before a smaller line of four people accepting condolences. Stan Lutz stood last, just before the casket; there was a dark wooden kneeler on the floor beside it. I watched as people reached to hug or shake the hands of the family members. I think the first two mourners were Mrs. Lutz's daughter and her husband. I couldn't remember the daughter's name and didn't recognize her husband. Or, I wondered, could it be the Lutzes had a son? Maybe the man was a Lutz son, not the husband of the daughter.

A pretty young woman with red eyes was third in line. She had a bunch of tissues in her hand and occasionally dabbed at tears, trying not to smudge her makeup, but her mascara had already run down from her left eye. Her breath would catch from time to time. I didn't know who she was but decided she was probably a granddaughter.

I watched Stan Lutz. He was a big man. His face was stoic, but his large body seemed to sag. He shook hands with each mourner, but occasionally his left hand reached behind him, groping for a surface to lean on. He shifted his weight back and forth. I worried he might stumble back. Someone had put a chair beside him, but I understood it would be hard for him to use it.

I didn't know what I was going to say when I got to the line of mourners. First in line was the Lutz daughter, and suddenly her name came to me.

"I'm sorry about your mother, Claire."

She took my hand in both of hers. "Thank you for coming, Sam."

Then she looked to the next person in line. So I reached out to shake the hand of her husband or brother. We both simply nodded.

Up close, the Lutz granddaughter's distress was plain. Her whole face was red and swollen. I took her hand. It was small and cold. I was afraid to squeeze it. I wanted to put my arms around her, but I could only say, "I'm sorry."

Stan Lutz's suffering made my chest ache. When we shook hands, he held on to me. We didn't speak, but I reached with my left hand to squeeze his shoulder. In Vietnam, death made me angry; here, I just felt sad.

The line was slow because most people stopped to kneel by the coffin for a prayer. Most knelt briefly, but one woman stayed there for a couple of minutes and seemed deep in prayer. I hadn't prayed in years, so I stood with my head bowed. My prayer was simple: *Please help the Lutz family.*

It didn't seem right to leave right away, so I moved to the other side of the crowded room and stood against the wall. Almost right away, someone grabbed my arm with a tight grip.

"Hello, tough guy." It was my wrestling coach, Jim Sweeney. Back in high school, he always called me "tough guy." I remember thinking he was mocking me when he first started using that nickname but later understood he meant it as a compliment.

"Coach! How are ya?" He still had a mean look, but I had experienced his soft side too. He knew how to comfort me when I lost a match. "I hear you're still coaching."

"I am. Hope to keep it up for a few more years. Not sure about next year's team, though. I'm not likely to have any state champions, but we'll have a decent chance to win the local league title. I don't have guys as good as you were, Sam. You were one of the best I ever had."

"Thanks, Coach; I appreciate that."

"It's true. And it's good to see you here. There's no reason you would know, but I was worried about you. A lot of folks were worried," he said.

"Worried? Why?"

He looked at me with a half smile. "C'mon, Sam. You were holed up in that cabin, drinkin' yourself goofy for months."

I laughed. "I didn't know you knew."

"You had a lot of folks worried."

"Really? I didn't know."

"I go to Allen's Beer Distributor to pick up a case of Yuengling every Friday. They were delivering so much of that stuff to you that one week they ran out, and I had to get another brand."

Now I felt embarrassed. "You're joking, right?"

"I'm joking a little, Sam. I was always able to get my Yuengling. But it's no joke that folks worried about your hermit lifestyle and beer consumption. This is a small town in a lot of ways, and we understood what you'd been through."

Suddenly, I was irritated. "What did I go through?" I could hear the anger in my voice.

Coach was stunned; I could see it on his face. "I'm sorry, Coach. I know folks were worried. I just had to be alone."

"No apology needed, Sam. You're right. We didn't really understand what you'd been through. We were worried, though, afraid you wouldn't heal. I know it was hard."

I had another lump in my throat and worried that a tear might slip out of my watery eyes.

"But it's great to see you back with us. How's the job? Do you like being an electric man?"

I smiled. "I really like it. It's a great job for me."

"Good. Why don't you come by and see me at the gym? We still practice in the same place. I know the kids would love to meet you. They all know about you. There's still a picture of you and several of your old medals in the trophy case in the main lobby of the high school." He paused. "They know about Vietnam too."

I was speechless again.

"Think about it," Coach said. "Now I'm going to talk to Stan." He thumped me on the shoulder. "Don't be a stranger." I watched him go directly to Stan Lutz and hug him.

I didn't go to Vera Lutz's funeral service at the Lutheran church the next day, even though my boss told me I could take the time off if I wanted. But going to Vera Lutz's wake was a milestone. I thought about it a lot, especially my talk with Coach. I was comforted to hear that folks in the community were concerned about me. I felt a little lighter, less lonely, like I was in the right place and doin' okay. In a way, it was a new homecoming.

A few months later, I accepted Coach's invitation to go to wrestling practice at the high school. But that's another story.

Holly

I'm an early baby boomer, born in 1946, when growing up in the Minisink Valley was peaceful. I'm an only child too, blessed with a happy childhood and good looks. But from 1965 to 1975, things were difficult. Now, I understand how my lack of confidence made things harder—didn't recognize I could make my own choices. I was well into my twenties before I started trusting my own instincts.

As a girl, I was a tomboy: didn't care much for dolls and loved playing boy's games. I could keep up with them too, although I was cursed with a girl's throwing motion. Hard as I tried, my throws all had an arc on them, so they were easy to hit. I'll bet if I'd had some coaching, I could've thrown a hard fastball.

I could beat most of the boys in a footrace, though. One time I beat Bobby Fields. Bobby was two years older than me and one of the best athletes in our school. I don't think he knew I was a fast runner, so by the time he realized, I had a big lead, and he couldn't catch me. They teased Bobby about it for years. If he hadn't died young from a brain tumor, they'd still be teasing him.

Things changed when I grew boobs—and they came early. It was an awkward time when I was thirteen. The boys I played with started treating me differently, and older boys noticed me. So I found girls to hang out with and started paying attention to makeup and clothes. I had a knack for making myself look good, and I enjoyed the lusty looks I got from the boys. I began dating when I was a freshman in high school but didn't have a steady boyfriend until my junior year. I have two big regrets from those years. I didn't recognize the value of higher education, so I never considered college, and I married Mark Kober.

Mark seemed like he had everything: good looks and a new 1963 Chevy Bel Air convertible that was bright red. Everyone looked when we drove around town with the top down in that car. I felt glamorous.

Mark's father was a county commissioner and owned a land-development company. Right out of high school, my future father-in-law got me a job in the county office. I'm a good worker, like to work, and have a knack for seeing what needs to be done. So even though I was young with limited experience, when the office manager retired, they gave me her job. I was only twenty years old.

That's when I became aware of the trouble being caused by the Tocks Island Dam. Before then, the dam wasn't something I paid attention to. I had known a few students in high school who were forced to move when the Army Corps of Engineers condemned their land. One of them was my friend Edie Waters. She moved away with her family—I'm not sure where to. Adult talk about the dam didn't interest me. My family didn't have to move, so I ignored the disruptions caused by the land condemnations. But when I started answering the telephone at the county commissioners' office, I found out about the hardships firsthand.

One situation, especially, sticks in my mind. Mrs. Schultz, a widow about seventy years old, lived off River Road about ten miles north of town. The Army Corps condemned her house for the Tocks Island Dam and forced her to sell. I forgot what they paid for her house, but it wasn't much. She didn't have any family in the area. She would call the office every few days, usually in tears. She was lost—didn't know where to go. We finally found a nephew of hers up in Minnesota who agreed to have her move to his home, but I could tell he wasn't real happy about it. I haven't thought about Mrs. Schultz for years, but I wondered what happened to her for a long time.

A lot of local folks call our area "the Minisink" because we're in the Minisink Valley, located in the Pocono Mountains of northeastern Pennsylvania. The Minisink includes the towns of Stroudsburg and East Stroudsburg, but most of the area is rural and had lots of small- and medium-size farms. Tourism is important. There used to be several resorts that specialized in honeymoons. There was a big billboard on the road claiming that we were "Honeymoon Capital of the World." One time, some of the boys painted "FUCKING" over the word "HONEYMOON," so now the sign read, "Fucking Capital of the World." It caused traffic slowdowns on the road for a week until someone corrected it. But they simply papered over "FUCKING" with "HONEYMOON," so the correction was visible to everyone who knew what had happened for a long time afterward. Years later, we still laugh about that.

Part of the office manager's jobs was to prepare the agenda for the county commissioners' monthly meetings, take notes at the meeting, and write up the minutes. This gave me a good understanding of the impact of the Tocks Island Dam. The stories of folks who lost their homes were heartbreaking. I began to believe that the government was not doing right. That's the main reason why I did what I did to help those opposed to the dam in the early 1970s. But I'm getting a little ahead of myself.

Marrying Mark Kober was a big mistake, but I did get a crash course in making my own decisions from that short marriage. And our daughter, Rachel, has been a joy from the beginning.

Mark and I started dating in my junior year; he was a senior. It was his senior prom. That's the night we went from heavy petting to intercourse. It was in 1963, and I still have the pictures somewhere. It was thrilling. Mark was handsome and rich. Two years later we got married. Looking back, that period's a blur. I don't even recall Mark asking me to marry him or even that I wanted to marry him. We were having sex, but I wasn't pregnant, although it was pure luck because half the time, we didn't take precautions. I remember we talked about getting married, and the next thing I knew, we were. I'm sure I've just forgotten the details. It was a confusing time.

Within months of being married, I was having second thoughts. Mark's father, Leo, was a bully. He bullied his son—criticized him all the time. If Mark hadn't worked for his father in their land business, it may not have been so bad because we could have avoided him most of the time. But, as it was, Mark saw him every day or two. Today, I can see a pattern that developed early in our marriage: Leo would criticize Mark about something or other; Mark would get angry and take it out on me. He hit me once, but I put a stop to that right away. I got our biggest kitchen knife and told him I'd kill him if he did it again. I don't think I would have, but he knew I was serious, so after that, he just abused me verbally. His hollerin' was scary enough.

The verbal abuse made me feel as though I was in the wrong. Mark claimed I didn't take his side against his father, and it was true; I didn't usually say anything when his father berated him. I know now there wasn't much I could do, but it was complicated because Leo Kober was a county commissioner, and I had to deal with him at work. It was miserable all around. Within a year our marriage was unhappy. I don't recall our actual honeymoon or even much of that honeymoon phase everyone jokes about.

My father-in-law was involved in quite a few transactions from the land condemnations. He'd seen what was coming, bought land before it was condemned, and then sold it to the govern-ment. Most folks who were forced to sell their homes didn't get a good price, but Leo Kober did. It took me a while to figure out how he did it. But I'm getting ahead of myself again.

I left Mark three years after we married; Rachel was fourteen months old. I didn't have anywhere else to go, so we moved back to my mom's house. I wanted to keep my job as long as I could, so I tried hard not to alienate my father-in-law. I met with him the day I moved out and told him it was a temporary separa-tion while Mark and I worked things out, even though I knew our marriage was over. Leo was crazy about Rachel, so I assured him that he could see his granddaughter whenever he wanted. It bought me some time—until I filed for divorce. That's when things got ugly.

I knew my job was at risk when they took responsibilities for the county commissioners' meetings away from me and gave the task to a woman who worked for the court. They told me it was because she had experience recording legal proceedings, but I knew they were beginning to shrink my job. Sure enough, within six months I was unemployed.

When they forced me out of my job in the county commissioners' office, I decided to expose Leo Kober's shenanigans. It's a good thing I was young and naïve. If I hadn't been, I would not have taken them on. My father-in-law had a lot of power, and he used it to make things difficult for me.

While I was still working at the Monroe County Courthouse, I met Sam Kopco. I knew who Sam was from high school, but I'm not sure we ever talked back then. I first noticed Sam when he was the captain of the wrestling team. He had a sexy body—hard and sinewy; and when he wrestled, he was a little scary—like a mean snake the way he stalked his opponents and twisted them around. I don't think I ever saw him lose a match, although I know he did occasionally. Sam looked intense around the campus too, hardly ever smiled, although he was social and had a lot of friends. But we hung out in different crowds.

I'd heard he got wounded in Vietnam, but I didn't know any more than that. I went to the celebration they had for him when he came home. He didn't look good that day. He'd lost weight and sat on the stage with his head down. He seemed scared. Then one day I saw him at the courthouse. He looked impressive. He'd gotten bigger, and that hard, strong look he had in high school had returned. Sam isn't classic handsome; he's good looking in a raw kinda way, and there's something about his physicality that made me want to watch him. He moved gracefully but didn't seem like the snake I imagined when he wrestled. Now he seemed lighter, more like a dancer.

He looked at me that day and kept looking. Our eyes held each other's for a few seconds, and he nodded—had a slight smile at his mouth. I had a strong reaction from that encounter that I still recall. I felt intrigued but a little frightened—as if he'd be dangerous. From then on, I'd look for him whenever I moved around the courthouse.

I saw him again about a week later. We were walking in opposite directions in a long corridor. Our eyes locked again, and we slowed as we approached each other. He started to continue past me, so I stopped, and then he did so too. He didn't say anything, seemed as though he was looking for words.

So I said, "Welcome home."

Then he smiled, a full smile; his face shed that serious look. In all our time together, I don't think I saw Sam smile that way ten times. But I remember that first one.

"Thanks," he said. "I've been home awhile; I mean it's nice to be home." Then he shrugged, but he was still smiling. "I guess you work here," he said.

"I do. In the commissioners' office."

"I remember you from high school."

"That seems like a long time ago," I said.

His face got serious. "It was a long time ago."

Immediately, I felt sad. *He's sad*, I thought.

But Sam brightened up quickly. "I need to get a building permit. Do you know where that office is?"

"Sure. I'll show you."

We walked quietly for a few moments until Sam stopped and turned. He seemed at a loss for words until he blurted, "Are you married?"

I had to smile at his directness. "I am. For now. I'm separated."

He looked relieved. "Good," he said. "I mean, I'm sorry."

"Don't be sorry; I'm not."

"That's great. I mean, I'm glad you're not sorry."

Then he shrugged again. A gesture I came to understand meant *I understand, but I don't know how to say so.*

We reached the building permit's office by then. Sam stuck his hand out, and I took it. I was surprised his hand was not bigger, but it was thick and calloused.

"I'll see you again," he said. I walked away smiling, with a tingle I hadn't felt for a while.

Sam called me at the commissioners' office that same afternoon. He didn't beat around the bush.

"I'd like to see you again."

Sam's directness is jarring at times, but it's one of the things I most like about him. I'm usually direct too. "I'd like to see you, Sam, but I can't date yet. It could cause trouble."

"Oh…I'm sorry…when can you date?"

"I'm not sure. It could be a while."

He was silent.

I said, "You can call me if you like."

He took me literally and called the next day and the day after that. But it was difficult for me to have a conversation in the office, and I was still living with my mom. So I got his number and called

32

him every few days. It wasn't long before my desire to be with him overcame my caution.

We had a routine. He'd get some takeout, and we'd meet at the ARoma Italian-bakery parking lot out on Route 611 after I finished work. The ARoma parking lot was behind the bakery, shielded from the road. The store closed in midafternoon, so its parking lot was empty late in the day. I left my car there, and we drove to Sam's cabin together.

A few rituals gave our affair some sense of normality. We took a shower as soon as we got to the cabin. We called it "rinsing the world away." We showered, made love, had something to eat, and went back to bed for more lovemaking. Music was important for us. Sam was building a record collection—78 rpms in those days. I liked the Beatles, Diana Ross, Neil Diamond, Aretha Franklin, and some others. Sometimes after we made love, we'd just lie there listening to music, not talking. I still remember those peaceful moments. I was never happier.

One day, as we lay naked, Sam asked, "Any progress on your divorce?" I knew he was impatient to see my marriage ended so we could be together openly. I wished that too.

"Not really. My lawyer tells me I'm going to need patience. Mark is determined to fight for every dollar; he's trying to get his child-support payment reduced."

"Why? He doesn't need the money; the family's loaded." Sam had begun to be angry with Mark.

"I know, but he doesn't want me to have any of it. He'd like to keep me poor."

"He's a son of a bitch."

"Tell me about it."

We were quiet. The intimacy of our lovemaking lingered. The bedclothes were bunched at the foot of the bed; both pillows lay on the floor. Sam reached down to retrieve the pillows and slipped one under my head and put the other under his.

"You know what I'm worried about?" I asked.

"What?"

"My job. I think Mark's father is looking for an excuse to get rid of me."

"They wouldn't know what to do without you."

I hesitated. I hadn't told anyone about Leo Kober's suspicious land deals. "I think he's worried about when I become his ex-daughter-in-law. I'm aware of some shady activities about land condemnations for the Tocks Island Dam."

"What'd they do?" he asked, turning toward me.

"Mark's father fiddled with the tax-assessment records. He bought land the Corps was about to condemn and recorded an inflated purchase price."

"So that meant they got a higher price when they sold it to the government?"

"Right." I'd begun wondering whether I should create trouble for the Kobers. I continued, "I'm not sure how much Mark knows about the fake records, but his father is in it up to his eyeballs."

"Seems to me the old man would want you to be happy. If I were him, I wouldn't want an unhappy daughter-in-law who knows about my dirty laundry."

"That's what I've been thinking," I said. "But the more I watch Commissioner Leopold Kober operate, I understand. He doesn't care about people—especially if you don't have clout."

"I'm not surprised."

"He's been cool to me lately, and I'd been thinking that it was just awkwardness because Mark and I split. Now, I'm worried."

"Are you afraid?" he asked.

"No. No, not physically afraid. But I'm nervous. I really need my job—at least until the divorce is final. I worry about money and taking care of Rachel by myself."

"Yeah, it would be hard to find another job as good as that one around here."

"Once I'm finished with Mark Kober and his family, I can get out of Dodge."

Sam's reaction was immediate. "You wouldn't leave me, would you?"

I understood Sam's reaction, but a realization had been taking hold: I might be smart to move when the divorce was final. I moved closer so that our naked bodies touched. "Sam, I don't want to leave you. I'm just not sure what I'll do when the divorce is over, but I might be smart to get away from here. At least for a while."

"Why?" he pleaded.

"I'm suffocated here. I won't have a chance to be me if I stay."

I don't think Sam ever understood my need to leave Strouds-burg, so it was a problem for us when I left.

Mark Kober

I waited for my father to arrive for our regular Wednesday lunch meeting at the Mountain Inn. My father, Leo Kober, liked the privacy of the place; the hotel was isolated in the hills outside Stroudsburg, and the restaurant had small dining alcoves, where we lunched and discussed business. Dad tried to keep our land-development activities concealed because they often conflicted with his role as a county commissioner. He was late for this week's meeting.

The Mountain Inn was an elegant old hotel built in the 1890s to serve a wealthy clientele from New York City and Philadelphia during the summer months. The lower temperatures of the Pocono Mountains, especially the cool evenings, attracted the rich from these close-by cities then. They kept coming up through the 1920s, but by the time we were meeting there, its future didn't look promising. The hotel/restaurant had lost its wealthy clientele and seemed unlikely to remain a viable business. Its location outside town was inconvenient, with the cost of maintaining the old building high. But the owners were hanging on in the hope that the upcoming Tocks Island Dam and Delaware Water Gap National Recreation Area would bring hordes of tourists back.

I looked out across the broad expanse of lawn that fell away from the east-facing window. This year's cold spring had delayed the emergence of flowering trees and shrubs, but now everything was out. I tried to enjoy the bright colors and beautiful setting, but I was anxious. I almost always left my meetings with Dad pissed off.

I handled day-to-day activities for Timber Development, the Kober family business. The enterprise had its roots in the forestry company my great-grandfather, Rudolph Kober, started in the mid-1800s after emigrating from Germany. Our family became wealthy until overharvesting of the timber, the emergence of huge timber companies, and the growing popularity of tourism reduced the company's economic viability. Leopold Kober, my father, Rudolph's grandson, sold the business to a land conglomerate in the late 1950s, retained the company name, and refocused its efforts on buying and selling land. The Tocks Island Dam project enhanced Timber Development's opportunities as soon as Congress approved the dam project in 1962.

My father was one of the first to recognize the economic opportunities and started buying land even before the Army Corps of Engineers began its survey activities. He had inside information, so most of the land he bought turned out to be within the area condemned for the dam. In the few places where his acquisitions fell outside the immediate damsite, he thought the land was desirable for individuals hoping to build vacation homes with direct access to the huge recreational lake planned for the area.

My father showed up forty minutes late, around the time I finished my second bottle of beer. Dad ordered an extra dry Tanqueray martini from Wilma, our regular waitress. After Wilma brought his martini, he took a sip and asked, "What've you been doing this week?"

It sounded like an accusation.

"A couple of things. I've had the heavy equipment out clearing the Lutz land. The timber's been hauled off, the stumps removed. It'll be leveled by the end of the day today," I said. "We want to hold off on selling it, though, right?"

"Right. Just have them throw grass seed and straw down."

"They can probably finish that in a couple of days."

Dad consulted his notes. "How about those dilapidated cabins on the track just north of Shawnee?"

I felt more confident. "We should get to that next week."

"Anything new going on with the squatters?"

"Not really. They're out and about more, now that the weathers warmed up. They're planting. It's hard to tell what. Probably the same as last year: corn, squash, and beans. I think one of their goats had kids."

"Did you ever talk to that creep who seems to be in charge—what's his name?"

"Will Mead. I've talked to him. It's hard to get more than a yes or no from him. I stopped at his house a couple of weeks ago. His wife said he wasn't home, even though I'm sure he was."

"I wish we could get rid of those parasites." My father was furious that the squatters had not been evicted, but they weren't living on any of our land. The land they occupied had already been bought by the Army Corps of Engineers. Still, their camp there devalued our land, if there was much value to it without the dam.

"The feds will have to take the initiative," I observed. "It's their land they're living on."

"They graze their animals on some of our land, don't they?"

"Dad, we've been over this. Local law enforcement has their hands tied. The feds have jurisdiction."

"We pay a lot of taxes—local and federal."

"You know I can't do anything about it," I said. I picked at the label on my beer and finally said, "You're the one with influence around here. Why don't you do something?"

"Don't get smart with me, young man."

I didn't respond.

Wilma came to take our lunch orders. "We have freshly made pea soup today but no fish. They're not catching anything on the river, and Zeke won't pay the distributor's prices for the trucked-in fish."

"I think the river's water is still too cold for good fishing," Leo said. "I'll have a cup of pea soup and a ham sandwich on rye."

"I'll have a cheeseburger and French fries. And another Yuengling."

"Another drink for you, Mr. Kober?"

"No, thanks. I've got a meeting this afternoon. I can't drink all day like my son."

Wilma started to comment but stopped when she saw my scowl. "I'll put your orders in."

We were quiet. Dad perused his appointment book, flipping its pages back and forth. I sat uncomfortably staring out the window. My father finally broke the silence.

"I've heard there's some land for sale on the west side of River Road just north of Zion Lutheran Church. Do you know where I mean?"

"I think so. There's a 'for sale by owner' sign on the side of the road; it says two acres."

"I might want to buy it."

"Why?" I asked. "It's all mountainside. It'd cost a bundle to build a house there."

"I don't want to build a goddamn house!" His raised voice echoed through the mostly empty room. Realizing he'd lost his cool, he straightened his silverware and composed himself.

I didn't respond.

He continued, "I don't want to buy it under Timber Development's name."

I waited for Dad to say more.

"It'd make sense to deed it in the name of our LLC, but Holly's still listed as secretary of the company, isn't she?"

I saw an opportunity to discuss my divorce expenses. "Right, we need to get that divorce finalized."

"We? What do you mean 'we'? You need to take care of that."

"Dad, my lawyer's waiting for another payment."

"Well, pay him."

"I don't have the money; you know that."

"Then sell that boat. You shouldn't have bought it in the first place." Leo leaned forward and said, lowering his voice, "Sell the fuckin' boat."

"I tried..." My father didn't know the boat was financed to the hilt. If I sold it, and I hadn't had any interest from my classified ads, I'd barely get enough to pay it off.

I tried a different approach. I tried to sound confident. "I think Holly has a boyfriend."

Leo didn't respond; he just stared at me.

"Rachel is spending a lot of time with Holly's mom. And last weekend she mentioned 'Mommy's friend.'"

Leo showed more interest. "What did she say?"

"She wouldn't say much, but I'm pretty sure it's a man."

"Why do you say that?"

"I don't know. It's just a hunch." My confidence slipped away.

"I don't want to hear about your hunches."

I said no more and turned my attention to my food.

We finished our lunches in silence. I had hoped to get money for my lawyer, but I wasn't ready to deal with more criticism and didn't pursue the topic. We went our separate ways after lunch.

I remember that lunch because it was a turning point for me. I was miserable—frustrated working for my father and sad and angry about my pending divorce. It would be another couple of years before I could cut the cord and move away, but at lunch that day, I started turning in that direction.

I still had a long way to go. I had a new girlfriend, but I was still pissed at Holly. I tried to make things as hard as I could for her. Half the time I didn't pick up our daughter for visitation when I was supposed to, just to make things complicated for her. So, my daughter and I never had a strong bond. She invited me to her wedding a year or two ago, but I didn't go. I didn't want to be reminded of those times.

I worried about our company's land operations. Dad kept me in the dark about the details, especially finances, but I'd begun to recognize there were some questionable things going on. I was still naïve, but it gradually dawned on me that I might get caught up in illegal stuff. And, it makes me sad to say it, but I came to understand that my father might not protect me. I didn't think he'd throw me under the bus right away, but I believed his first instinct would be to protect himself.

Loretta Shuster

Until the government began condemning land in the Minisink Valley for a dam we didn't need, I was a young housewife and mother occupied with raising children, but when my parents were forced to sell their farm for an unfair price because it fell within the area that would be flooded by the Tocks Island Dam, I was aroused. Expulsion from his farm eventually killed my father, and his death, combined with the loss of their home, devastated my mother. Dad lived for his farm and his family, so when his farm was taken from him, he lost a part of himself. He lived several years after he was evicted, but they were unhappy years. Mother was never the same either, especially after Dad died.

At first, folks were excited about the Tocks Island Dam. But it gradually became apparent that the dam would change our lovely Minisink Valley in fundamental ways. The natural beauty of the free-flowing Delaware River would be destroyed; a quiet paddle down the river would no longer be possible. The dam would disrupt the shad migration. Loud motorized boats would zip about on the huge lake behind the dam and change the character of the place. New roads and buildings would be required to accommodate the millions of tourists projected to come to the area for recreation. By the late 1960s, the belief took root that our beautiful, quiet valley would be forever changed.

Most people in the Minisink are down-to-earth and clear eyed and work hard. They know injustice when they see it, but they're reticent too. The government's land grabs eventually broke through that reticence. My parents' case and a few others became emblematic and stoked a lot of anger in the community. At the time, the country was angry too. About Vietnam. About civil rights. About a lot of different things. Groups disagreed about what was wrong, so they were mad at one another too.

Anger at the land condemnations and worry about the environmental harm the dam would do laid the groundwork for people to mobilize. I came to understand that powerful interests were aligned to build the dam: federal, state, and local governments; electric-power companies; local businesses; and others. I was inexperienced and naïve about politics, but I decided to try to stop or at least modify the plans. It's a good thing I was naïve. If I had known the power of dam interests, I may not have taken them on.

I'm usually quiet, but I pay attention. Early on, I kept my opinions to myself—at least in public. But eventually I began to speak out. I was amazed at the number of people who listened, and for a while anyway, I was unnerved by the attention. But other people's encouragement motivated me. There was a need for strong local voices to express people's growing concerns about the dam. Eventually, my voice represented the views of many others, and I came to relish my role as a spokeswoman.

For a time, the Tocks Island Dam issue was an obsession and required a lot of my time. This upset my marriage. Problems popped up over the things I didn't do at home. For years, I'd been taking Paul's shirts and suits to be cleaned and pressed every week. One week I forgot, and usually patient Paul hit the roof. I bit my tongue and took the suits and shirts to the cleaners the next day. Then I got angry. After dinner one night when the dishes were done and the kids were doing homework, I brought up the household chores.

"I've got a lot going on with dam-opposition activities and trying to keep the house running. I'd like to have more help from you around here."

Paul didn't answer. He just stared back at me, the wrinkles between his eyebrows popped up. I could always tell when Paul was angry by his eyebrows. But I went ahead anyway.

"Would you take your own shirts and suits to the cleaners and pick them up?"

"Why?" he responded. Now his jaw was clenched too.

I could feel my stomach change from butterflies to knots. "Because I don't have the time."

"What makes you think I do? Besides, the cleaner isn't open when I go to work in the morning."

"They're open when you come home. You could drop them off and pick them up on your way home."

"Do you really need so much time for this Tocks Dam stuff?"

"Yes, I do! I limit my time on the Tocks activities as much as I can and still keep it going."

"Why don't you let someone else take the lead?"

47

My stomach was really in knots now, and I could feel my face getting hot. "Because I don't want to. And you could help a little too, you know."

He didn't respond; he just got up, and thirty seconds later, I heard the door to the garage slam. I was in bed, half asleep when he got home. I felt him get in bed, but I could tell he was way over on the other side.

Paul and I had never had a direct confrontation before the shirts, and it stayed frosty between us for a while. The dinner table was uncomfortable. The children knew something was wrong and stopped talking. I didn't take his stuff to the cleaners, and after a week, Paul started doing it himself. We never discussed the disagreement about his shirts, but after a couple of weeks, Paul started being more helpful. He did the weekly food shopping, and he'd help me fold laundry. He got much friendlier in bed too.

It took a few months, but eventually we developed a more cooperative arrangement. Occasionally I'd call him at work if I couldn't be home for dinner, and he'd cook for Jessie and Paul Jr.

Eventually Paul stepped into the spotlight more than me. I'm still a little uncomfortable as a public figure, but Paul is an open, friendly guy who enjoys being a greeter and schmoozer. This relieved me of a job that felt artificial.

I inherited a knack for detail from my father. Our land was marginal for farming: some sections were rocky, other parts boggy, and much of it hilly. I watched my father make the most of the land by the close attention he paid to crop selection, nourishing the land and modifying its contours. One day, early in high school, doing my algebra homework, I had an insight about the similarity between the rules required to solve equations and the care my father took with our land. I know the analogy is imperfect, but the lesson stayed with me. I recognize the value of considering things that may not be important by themselves but contribute to a solution. This habit served me well in school and was crucial for attacking the Tocks Dam plans. I know it irritates my husband and children when I remind them "the devil is in the details," so I don't say it very often.

I brought my knack for detail to the Tocks Island Dam issue. I'm one of a handful of local people who have read the Tocks enabling legislation and the voluminous technical materials from the Army Corps of Engineers. I also attended and took notes at public hearings associated with the dam. Early on, I was quiet at meetings, but as I filled my head with information and began to understand the big picture, I started asking questions and gradually understood the power of a sharp and timely question.

One day at a commission meeting, there was a complicated discussion going on about building the dam. I couldn't understand the technicalities. Nobody in the audience could. I suspected it was part of the strategy to keep the audience off-balance. But when an opportunity for questions came, I asked, "Why is it that in 1942, test borings done by the government determined that Tocks Island was not a suitable site for a dam and recommended that a dam be built at Wallpack Bend instead? What has changed since 1942?"

Well, you should have seen the look on the faces of the experts at the head table. I don't think most of them knew anything about a 1942 feasibility study. I'd discovered it in an appendix to a report from the Army Corps of Engineers. The "experts," heads down, began studying the papers in front of them. The chairman pretended he was looking for something in the thick folder in front of him. I think I saw a slight smile at the mouth of the guy sitting on the far left. It was hard not to laugh. The chairman finally said something about finding the old study and reporting back, and they adjourned the meeting.

Looking back, this criticism was a small milestone in our long effort to stop the dam. But I soon understood too that this and other small victories were not going to stop the dam. It had taken on a life of its own, and the "machinery" was moving steadily toward construction.

I was baffled by political and economic matters in the beginning. I believed most people were honest and that government acted in the interest of most citizens. I considered myself well informed and savvy enough to recognize that every government action doesn't benefit everybody. Inevitably, there are winners and losers; that's the price of living in society. But in the beginning, I failed to recognize the power of a few individuals with lots of resources and influence to shape what happens, regardless of whether it's generally a good thing.

I should say too that the movements of the late 1960s energized me even though I was and remain a pretty conservative Republican. I was in favor of the Vietnam War and, at least in the early years, thought the war protestors were damaging the war effort. I disapproved of the shenanigans of too many young people. They seemed mainly interested in sex, drugs, and challenging all kinds of authority; I couldn't see anything constructive in what they were doing. Time has shown the dissenters were right about Vietnam— fifty-eight thousand of our boys killed in a failed war. After a few years, the most flagrant of the sex-and-drug abuse faded some. Or at least I didn't see it on the front page every day.

As I look back, I can see the late 1960s liberated me, even though I'm not a women's libber. I started to recognize that many of the things I accepted without question were unacceptable. Environmental issues captured my imagination, and at the top of my environmental damage list was the Tocks Island Dam.

My conversion from housewife to activist took a while, but when it took hold, I was effective, if I do say so myself. Aside from raising two children, helping to kill the Tocks Island Dam is my biggest accomplishment. That experience had a lasting effect too. I stayed active politically for many years.

My anti-Tocks activities spiced up my life too. I got to know some interesting people, and a few of them became friends. I developed a knack for figuring out what people want and a fascination with how they go about trying to get it. Personal styles are often amusing and, unfortunately, sometimes appalling.

The smartest thing I did was establish the Lower Minisink Environmental Defense group. There were some individuals concerned about protecting the Delaware Water Gap area's natural environment, and several of us started getting together at my house. We weren't formally organized in the beginning, but after three or four of our get-togethers, we decided to formalize things. We wrote what today they call a "Mission Statement." I haven't seen that statement for years, but as I recall, it talked mainly about the environmental damage the dam would cause. We used the term "environmental defense" on purpose in the hope that we would attract the attention of others passionate about protecting the valley. We elected "officers." director—me; secretary-treasurer—Elizabeth Pope, an assistant principal at the high school; and publicity—Fred Dugan, a retired banker. We felt a little silly at first having a formal organization because we were only a handful of members with no money and not even a clear idea of what to do.

We had a printer-make stationery with a nice letterhead showing our names and positions at the top, and then we sent letters about our concerns to everyone we could think of: our senators and congressmen, local politicians, the Army Corps of Engineers, the Delaware River Basin Commission, and others. I can't remember them all. Gradually, over a year or two, folks started paying attention; eventually they allowed us to speak at meetings. A couple of times, the county commissioners even asked our advice.

We got involved to save Sunfish Pond, a forty-acre pond in a picturesque setting at the top of Kittatinny Mountain on the New Jersey side of the river. There was a proposal from several power companies to use the pond site for a large pumped storage facility that would have resulted in the destruction of the pond. We worked with other groups to organize opposition that brought about the cancellation of the power company's plan. Key to our effort was a demonstration at Sunfish Pond attended by William O. Douglas, an associate justice of the US Supreme Court. I think Douglas's involvement, which attracted extensive newspaper and television coverage, was the thing that saved Sunfish Pond.

We had difficulties along the way, of course. An early challenge arose when Mark Kober asked to join our group. Mark was the son of Leo Kober, a county commissioner and land developer. He was in his late twenties at the time and worked for his father's land-development company. He was a dapper-looking young man.

Unlike most businessmen in the area who wore dark suits and conservative neckties, Mark dressed smartly, favoring tan slacks, light-blue broadcloth shirts, and a dark-blue blazer. His shoes were always shined and his hair cut neatly. He was average height with Germanic good looks—blond hair and eyebrows, pale-blue eyes, with a broad forehead. These cosmetic strengths gave way at his rounded chin, which contrasted with the angularity above. Mark had trouble as a teenager—had an automobile accident that killed his passenger. I'd heard too that he developed a drug problem when he went away to college down in Philly that got so bad that it forced him to drop out.

At first, we were happy to have Mark join us, hopeful that we might gain some influence with his father. But after he came to a couple of meetings, we began to suspect that he was not opposed to the dam and was representing his father's interests. Things came to a head at an early meeting.

Fred Dugan brought up the "for or against" the dam issue. Fred was an active member of the original group. He was raised in the Minisink, left for a thirty-five-year career at an investment bank in New York City, and had recently moved back to the small community of Dingmans Ferry, an unspoiled area north of where the dam was to be built. Almost immediately upon his return, Fred got involved in opposition to the dam.

The meeting in my living room had just begun when Fred observed, "I think momentum is shifting in our direction. Dam supporters have gone quiet. The public mood is hostile. The farmers and homeowners have gotten over the shock of being thrown off their land and are angry." He let this sink in and then asked, "Is that the way you see it, Loretta?"

"I agree that folks are angry," I said, "but I don't agree momentum has been reversed. All the money and power is on the other side. Millions of dollars are at stake. Local and state governments are still pushing for construction, and a lot of local businessmen are in favor."

I looked directly at Mark Kober, who diverted his eyes.

The room was quiet, and the clock on my mantle dinged once, accentuating the silence.

Elizabeth Pope, the assistant high-school principal, broke the silence. "I agree with Loretta. We need to keep the pressure up. Recruit more people to our cause. We should hold our local politicians to account. In fact, I don't know where most of them stand. I imagine most of them would like to see the dam built for its economic benefits, but they've gone quiet." She then looked pointedly at Mark, who stayed quiet.

I started to address Mark directly about his thoughts but changed my mind. I tried to steer the meeting to planning future activities, but Fred wouldn't let Mark off the hook and asked him directly.

"What does your father think about all this?"

Mark hesitated and then spoke. "He sees a lot of economic potential. Dam construction will create jobs while it's being built and bring thousands of tourists when it's complete." His voice trailed off.

Fred Dugan raised his voice. "Who's going to pay for the new roads we'll need? The additional police? The expanded infrastructure to support the inevitable commercial development?"

Mark didn't answer.

I looked around the room, and it seemed clear these concerns resonated with all except Mark.

We moved on to other topics: letter writing to state and federal authorities, attempts to recruit residents to the cause, development of a pamphlet raising questions about the dam, and plans to have a booth at Stroudsburg's annual Fourth of July celebration.

When the meeting adjourned an hour and a half later, Fred Dugan stayed behind to have a word. "What do you think about Mark Kober attending our meetings?"

"It's a bad idea," I replied. "I'm sure he's reporting our plans to his father."

"I agree. How do we get rid of him?"

"I'll call him. Tell him frankly we think he might be on the other side, and that he shouldn't come to meetings if he's not willing to support our cause. I'll be nice, but I bet he won't come again. In fact, I'll stop sending him notices about upcoming meetings. And we won't send him a summary of this meeting."

"That should do it."

"I may hear from his father, but I can handle him."

Fred smiled. "I'm sure you can."

Mark did stop coming to our meetings.

After the successful Sunfish Pond episode, we started attracting new members. Most were women, but one young man was important to our activities. Sam Kopco. Sam was a Vietnam veteran who worked for the power company. I didn't know him personally, but he was a state wrestling champion in high school, and I had vivid memories of the community celebration when he came home after Vietnam. There was a lot of publicity about the homecoming because Sam had initially been reported missing in action; the Pocono Record reported his MIA status on the front page.

About a week later, we got notice he was alive but wounded. He was our first local casualty. He was hospitalized for months. When he finally came home, Stroudsburg had a big celebration.

I remembered watching Sam's discomfort on the stage at the celebration. Our high-school marching band was there; flags and balloons were out all up and down Main Street. Most of all, I remember Sam's distress during the politicians' speeches. He didn't look well; he'd had several surgeries and was gaunt, worn out. You could tell he did not want to be up on that stage. I was afraid he would leave abruptly during the ceremonies and understood how embarrassing that would be for him and the town fathers. I prayed for Sam that day—held my breath hoping God would help him stay in his seat. He did, although he bolted right after the last word was spoken, avoiding all the people who had wanted to say a word to him.

Adding to everyone's discomfort that day were three hippie types, students from East Stroudsburg State, at the back of the crowd with homemade "Stop the War" signs. At the start of the ceremony, one of them started to shout out antiwar slogans. The mayor was speaking at the time; he stopped talking immediately. The crowd got so quiet that it was scary. The demonstrator stopped hollering right away too. It was a good thing. I think everyone felt like demonstrating at that gathering was a desecration. The demonstrators didn't leave, but they were quiet after that. I think they understood they were in danger if they kept on.

I didn't recognize Sam when he came to his first meeting with us. It had only been a couple of years since his homecoming, but he looked very different: heavier, stronger looking, and not scared and nervous. His face and demeanor were calm. At first, I wasn't sure why he joined us; he was quiet at meetings, but then we learned he had a lot of firsthand information about the land that was condemned from his job with the power company. Most of the land was in his territory, and he knew a lot about the eminent domain land condemnations.

It was soon clear that Sam favored what we were trying to do. He liked the outdoors and worried that the Minisink's hunting, fishing, canoeing, and hiking assets were threatened by the dam. Eventually we discovered that his girlfriend worked for the county commissioners and knew about some financial shenanigans around the land transfers. This information proved useful later when things turned in our direction.

We had another tricky membership issue early on. Will Mead was the "mayor" of Cloud Farm, the hippie community that occupied some of the land bought by the Army Corps of Engineers. Those hippies might have called it a community or a commune or whatever, but we locals called them "squatters," and that was that.

Will shared our goals and wanted to join the group, but if we had accepted Will, it would have been a public-relations problem given the locals' animosity toward the squatters. They were living on real estate taken from our friends and neighbors, so there was a widespread hostility. They didn't fit in either. Most of the men had long hair and beards, and the women dressed like gypsies. There were all kinds of rumors about drug use and free sex up there on the river north of town. I didn't believe half of what people said, but we decided we couldn't have them in Lower Minisink Environmental Defense. They'd compromise our credibility with the officials we were trying to influence—officials who had been trying for some time to evict them from their settlement.

The first time he came to see me at home, I was scared. He had a presence. Intense, deep-set eyes that gleamed like droplets of oil; long black hair and a thick black beard. He was short, wiry. Nothing at all like the voice I'd heard on the phone. I was reluctant to invite him in that first time he showed up. If I hadn't recognized his voice, I'm sure I would've sent him away and locked the door behind him. It wasn't until the next year I realized what frightened me so about him. The first time I saw Charles Manson on the news, I saw that same intensity, that same charisma, but Will lacked that little spark of crazy that lived in Manson's eyes. Still, I shudder to think of it today.

I never quite adjusted to the contrast between Will's appearance and his understated demeanor. He was intelligent and articulate and had a sophisticated understanding of the politics surrounding the controversy. I soon found out he had a Ph.D. in Sociology and had hoped to set up a self-sustaining, model community he called Cloud Farm—one based on "back to the earth" environmentally friendly, cooperative living principles.

Will's main purpose for wanting to join our cause was to stop the dam. Cloud Farm would end up under water if the dam was built. But he also understood that his group was viewed with hostility by almost all the locals. He and I agreed to talk occasionally about issues of mutual interest, especially environmental ones. He also asked that I alert him to any plans to evict his group. As I look back, I think Will understood that his experiment to establish the kind of community he had in mind was doomed in its present location and circumstances, but many in his community were still determined and hopeful. There were also quite a few in his community who were "deadbeats," to use my husband's description, which is to say they enjoyed the hippie lifestyle, liked being outsiders. I think Will saw that it was his role to bring his constituents around to the realization that their dream would not survive the strong opposition they were seeing in the Minisink.

I was frank with Will about our interests and the community's unfriendly views toward his group. But on a few occasions, I found his observations useful. He had a better sense of the political realities than I did. I'm not sure I was much help to him, though. Once or twice I warned him about the upcoming attempts to evict his people, and they got restraining orders from the court. But when the final, forceful eviction came before dawn on a bitterly cold February morning, I'd had no advance information. The squatters were evicted by a well-planned large force that had managed to keep their operation secret until they launched it.

There were times when I thought we were doomed to get the dam. I began to be optimistic when the US attorney's office brought fraud charges against Leo Kober, but before that happened, there were times when my parents needed attention, and I had difficulties juggling the demands of my family and the environmental defense group.

Jack Neumann

I sat in my office on the tenth floor of the US Army Corps of Engineers regional headquarters in downtown Philadelphia, waiting for a call I knew would be difficult. My boss in Washington, General Matt McWilliams, was unhappy about the progress of the Tocks Island Dam, one of only a few large ongoing Corps initiatives. As the director of the Philadelphia region, I was responsible for the Pocono Mountain area of northeastern Pennsylvania.

I had a great office during those difficult years. To the east I saw the classical architecture of the main branch of the Free Library of Philadelphia on Logan Square. The building reminded me of many I saw in Europe when I traveled there after college. From the south-facing window, I had an unobstructed view of Philadelphia City Hall with its "Second Empire" French architecture. Even after viewing City Hall for several years, I still saw details in the complex and ornate building I hadn't noticed before. Just sixty years earlier, at the turn of the twentieth century, City Hall was the tallest occupied building in the world. I had an interest in early American history, so the scene out from my office windows fed my sense of having a part in the continuing development of the country. But the Tocks Island Dam project and the broad unrest roiling the country had begun to erode my optimism.

My buzzer sounded. "General McWilliams is on the line."

I took a deep breath and picked up the receiver. "Good morning, General."

"I haven't gotten the revised geology report yet." He sounded angry.

I took another deep breath. "General, the geologists are not going to modify their conclusions. I talked to them again last week. They're dug in."

"Then take out that final section."

I hesitated. "Where do I get the authority for that?"

"You already have the authority. You're the project director."

"General, with respect, this is not a simple administrative or operational decision. It bears on the viability of the entire project."

I envisioned the general's demeanor: red-faced, leaning forward over his desk, fist clenched. I knew he was tempted to order: *Just fuckin' do it!* But he also understood the risks that order posed. I would document in the files that General McWilliams ordered dam construction go forward despite adverse findings in the geologist's assessment. If problems developed later, responsibility would end up in the general's lap.

He ignored my point about viability. "I've already had a call from Senator Pike's office. And I'll bet I hear from the New York and Pennsylvania governors' offices before long. Shafer's office calls us every couple of weeks complaining about delays."

"I understand the problem, General. But we can't ignore a finding that could result in catastrophic failure."

"That exaggerates the risk."

I didn't respond.

"Look," the general sounded conciliatory now, "how about you have the subcontractor start digging. Then at least I'll have some construction progress to report. It'll keep the hounds at bay for a while."

"I can do that, General, but I need more money. Once I order the excavation contractor to begin work, the available dollars will be gone in two months. In fact, I probably won't have enough to pay their second month's bill."

"Yeah." The general was exasperated. "Our funding is stuck in appropriations, and I'm afraid they're going to reduce it further. This fucking war is sucking all the money out of the system."

"It's a problem," I agreed.

"Okay," McWilliams said. "Keep your ear to the ground and try to head off negative publicity, especially from the goddamn squatters."

I was troubled by the Tocks Island Dam project. I'd had technical reservations about the suitability of the Tocks Island site for some time, and the recent geological analysis by a panel of experts had not been reassuring. Ice-age activity over thousands of years had created unstable conditions as deep as two hundred feet that, over time, could compromise the stability of the dam structure. Digging down to solid, stable ground would increase the cost by 40 percent and delay completion by months, maybe a year. On top of that, the environmentalist's opposition posed a new threat to the construction. I was beginning to doubt whether the dam would be built. But powerful federal, state, and local interests were determined to push forward.

I'd been in the hot seat for a couple of years. Pressure from the Corps headquarters, three state governments, a growing environmental movement, and a variety of local interests kept me under constant stress with conflicting agendas. My request for a transfer to the Corps' Tulsa Oklahoma district, where there was less political intrusion, had been denied.

I hadn't told the general about the recent death in Stroudsburg. A woman had committed suicide. She had been forced from her long-term family home when we used eminent domain to buy her land. In fact, I was lucky to have learned about it. I no longer had my people at the damsite, as surveying and land-condemnation stages were almost complete. The absence of eyes and ears on the ground kept me in the dark about local happenings. I'd subscribed to the local newspaper. That's how I learned about the Lutz woman's suicide. But I needed more if I hoped to be alerted to trouble before it happened.

I worried about the environmentalists. They were causing real trouble. They'd won some local people over and had managed to generate national attention. US Supreme Court Justice, William O. Douglas, had come to the area about a year earlier to demonstrate in support of the environmental cause.

I had an idea. My father, Bart Neumann, was a retired Pennsylvania State Police detective. Dad spent thirty-two years with the Pennsylvania State Police, the first twelve patrolling the state's highways but the last twenty in the investigative division. My parents had retired to rural and historic Bucks County, where Dad had spent the last decade as a state-police detective. He was only an hour's drive from the Delaware Water Gap.

I checked my watch; it was nearing noon, and I'd heard Mom complain that since his retirement, Dad always seems to be underfoot at midday mealtime.

I dialed my parents' home. "Good morning, Dad. How's it going?"

"Jack! How are you?"

"I'm good. How's Mom?"

"She's good too. Except she's not used to having me around so much. She gets a little cranky."

I laughed. "I'll bet she'd say you're the cranky one."

"Yeah, probably. What's up?"

"You remember the Delaware River dam project I'm working on, don't you?"

"I think so."

"We're building a dam across the Delaware above the Water Gap. It's going to be called the Tocks Island Dam. Some day when we have an hour, I'll tell you the whole story. For now, I'll just say the project is threatened by local opposition, environmentalists, and a shortage of money. I'm getting a lot of heat from my boss in Washington, who is getting a lot of heat from the people he has to keep happy."

"I hear you. Shit flows downhill."

"I'd like to keep up with local developments, but I don't have people on the ground anymore, and there are signs of trouble. The wife in one of the families that we forced off their land killed herself. It could cause trouble."

"That's too bad—about the wife, I mean."

"I know. They were the third generation living on the land we condemned."

"I understand you've got to do your job, Jack. But that's gotta make you feel lousy."

"It does." We were quiet for a moment, and then I continued, "What do you think about going up there and snooping around? Try to figure out if I've got more trouble coming."

"Sure. I'd enjoy poking around up there. It's a beautiful time of year, and I think I can help. It'll be fun."

A few days later, my father called me at the office first thing in the morning. "I talked to several people up by the Delaware Water Gap and have a report for you. Can I come by there this afternoon or tomorrow morning?"

"Sure. You have information for me?"

"Yeah. A lot. Too much for a phone call."

"Okay. This afternoon's not good, but tomorrow's fine."

"What time do you get there in the morning?"

"Around eight, but how about we talk over lunch?"

"I'll get there around noon."

"Great. I'll see you tomorrow."

I hung up feeling concerned by my father's businesslike tone, and as I discovered the next day, my concern was justified.

Instead of having Dad come to my office, we decided to meet for lunch at the original Bookbinders restaurant at second and Walnut in downtown Philly. Dad loved that restaurant. It had a long history and a historical decor: the Gettysburg Address was posted by the front door. The first few lines of the Declaration of Independence: "We hold these truths to be self-evident that all men are created equal..."were painted in big letters on the ceiling in the main dining room. Photographs of the first thirty-nine US presidents adorned the walls.

Lobster was the main reason he loved Bookbinders; they had the largest indoor lobster tank in the world. It could hold 350 lobsters. I figured it was going to be an expensive lunch for me; Dad would probably order a whole lobster. Somehow, he had gotten the idea that I made a lot of money. I earned a good living but not as much as he thought.

I decided beforehand to enjoy this time with my father; he was good company and a great storyteller. I was anxious to discover what he found out up in the Minisink too. Mom told me he'd spent the better part of three days up there, so I was sure he'd gotten a lot of information. I knew firsthand from my teenage years about his knack for getting more information from you that you wanted to give.

Dad was at a table in the back of the restaurant when I arrived. He looked energized. I had seen him about a month earlier and was concerned that he seemed depressed, not his usual animated self. I had wondered if the inactivity of retirement was bad for him.

He grabbed me in a bear hug and kissed me on the cheek. "Great to see you, Jack. It's not often enough."

"I agree. But the weeks fly by, and the kids always seem to have something going on."

"I understand. I do. It's not all your fault. Your mom and I can get in the car and come to you. I've made a promise to myself that I'm going to come down this year to see Danny's basketball games."

"He'd love that, Dad."

Our waiter came and stood by our table, pad and pencil ready.

Dad looked at me. "I'd going to have a Wild Turkey on the rocks. Will you join me?"

"I'll have a Heineken."

The waiter nodded and turned to leave.

"Add a couple of lemon peels to that Wild Turkey."

The waiter nodded again without a word.

Dad watched him walk away. "He must be from New York," he said.

Then he turned back to me, paused, took a deep breath, and looked me in the eye. The joviality was gone from his voice. "Things are a mess up in the Poconos."

I wasn't ready for his stark assessment. "Really—about the dam?"

"Let me ask a couple of questions before I go on," he said.

"Sure."

"Is the Army Corps of Engineers finished taking land for this Tocks Dam?"

"We should be. When our site preparation gets further along, we may have to condemn a little more acreage, but we don't think so." I felt a need to say, *We don't* take *the land, Dad; we buy it,* and somehow justify our actions.

Dad nodded and went on. "How come you're letting all those hippie squatters live on the Corps' land?"

I felt defensive. "I know. That's a problem. We need to get those people moved, but there's bureaucratic infighting going on."

"How so?"

"Well, the Corps negotiated leases to rent some of the land we bought, but we had no idea the people who leased the land were going to bring a bunch of other people with them. Then after a couple of months paying their rent, they quit paying. It's not a problem for me now, so I haven't checked to see where things stand. I know our Contracts Office that signed the leases has been trying to get our lawyers to evict the squatters for nonpayment of rent, but as I understand it, they ignore the eviction notices, and there is a disagreement over how to evict them. The Corps' enforcement folks don't have the manpower to carry out an eviction. They've been trying get the FBI and local law enforcement to help, but for some reason, that hasn't happened. So far, I've been happy to let others worry about it. It's not likely to bite me on the ass, and, frankly, I don't want to get sucked into a messy situation that I had nothing to do with."

"I see," Dad said thoughtfully. "I understand bureaucratic infighting, but the squatters are one of the reasons why folks up there are pissed. Seems to me, most folks are opposed to building a dam, or at least *this* dam. Even if you get it built, I wouldn't be surprised if someone didn't blow it up."

"Really? I didn't know. I know there's some dissatisfaction about our use of eminent domain to buy land, but that's often an issue. The reality is that it's hard for folks to do anything to stop it."

"Do you know how much you're paying people for their land?"

"No, not for individual parcels…"

"Wait a minute, Jack. Don't you have to approve the amounts people get for their homes?"

"No, not for individual parcels. A separate office handles those details. I'm aware of our budget for acquisition, and when I review the monthly financial reports, we seem to be on target in that budget category. We'll probably need more than we budgeted, but that's usually the case. The acquisitions line item is hard to estimate ahead of time. We usually end up having to get a supplement to the budget. It's true that people often feel they didn't get a fair property for their property. They tend to think it's worth more than it is."

"No wonder they feel ripped off."

Dad stared at me. I didn't respond.

The silence hung heavy in the air.

Finally, he said, "I think you should go up there, Jack."

I felt defensive, didn't understand Dad's bluntness. "What can I do at this point? We don't have the money to move ahead with the construction right now. I'm waiting for an additional financial commitment."

Dad was quiet, head down. "Are you in charge of the project?"

"Well, yes, but my hands are tied until I get more money."

"Who will take the fall if the dam doesn't get built?"

"Well, I wouldn't get all the blame, but it'd definitely be a black mark."

"You know this business better than I do, Jack, but it sure looks like a white elephant to me."

Dad went on to describe the discontent he found. I was gloomy when he finished. I don't even recall if he had lobster for lunch.

A few days later, I decided to take Dad's advice and go up to the Minisink to see things for myself, but I was still unclear about the situation, so I decided to stop by Mom and Dad's on my way to get more input from Dad. I got to their house early, and Mom had a full breakfast ready, including my favorite breakfast meat: scrapple.

I love scrapple. The joke about it is that you don't want to know what's in it. My argument is that it's the same as sausage, and you don't want to know what's in that either. But my wife won't cook scrapple, says it stinks up the house, and it's a little tricky to cook without it falling apart, so I quit buying it—hasn't been in my refrigerator at home for years. It was delicious that morning.

After breakfast, Dad and I went down to his basement workshop to talk.

"So, what are you going to do when you get up to Stroudsburg?" he asked.

"Well, I was going to drive around and look at the damsite and go to see where the squatters are living to start, but I'm hoping you'll have some suggestions for me."

"I do. But let me tell you more about who I talked to."

"Great."

"First thing I did was to go see a state-trooper friend of mine up at the Hazleton barracks. He's been workin' the Minisink Valley area for years. He didn't know a lot about your dam, but he knew generally what was goin' on."

"I'm all ears."

"He knows about the hippie squatter problem and the general unrest. But he told me a couple of other things that got my investigative nose twitching."

"Woke up your cop instincts, huh?"

"You could put it that way. Anyway, he said that he'd been told by state-police headquarters to pass any information that came to him about the dam directly to them. They wanted to approve anything he might do in that connection. That request came directly from the governor's office in Harrisburg. They're determined to see that this dam gets built but worried about how things are going."

"Did he know what they're worried about?" I asked.

"Not specifically, but Harrisburg is afraid of growing political unrest, and my friend thinks there has been illegal activity involving a land company over there. He didn't think the squatters were a big problem—figured once the decision was made to get them off the land, it'd be a quick operation."

"That's good," I observed, "about the squatters, I mean."

"Yeah. But the other stuff, criminal activity and the growing local opposition—that sounds more serious."

"Okay," I said, still not feeling like I understood.

"My friend suggested I go see two people over in the Minisink for starters, the Stroudsburg police chief and a guy who owns a popular local watering hole, the Village Tavern. That's what I did.

"I went to see the chief first. Name's Ben Detweiler. I knew the name but had never met him. He's a lifelong resident of the Minisink, a local hero because his high-school basketball team won a state championship. He went to college locally at East Stroudsburg and was a leading scorer on their basketball team. You wouldn't know he was an athlete by looking at him today, but he's a nice guy. He knew what was goin' on with the dam, of course, but I could tell he wasn't all that anxious to discuss details. But he remembered me from my involvement in the takedown of a gambling operation up there years ago, so he answered most of my questions."

"Do you think he'll talk to me?"

"I think so. In fact, he may be happy to have a conversation with someone with direct involvement in the dam construction."

"Good. How about the guy at the Village Tavern?"

"He'll be a fountain of information, as long as you don't ask him to discuss individuals. Bartenders don't share customers' secrets."

By the time I got to Stroudsburg, it was almost noon. Dad had called ahead to tell Chief Detweiler I was coming, so the chief's secretary showed me into his office as soon as I arrived. We sat at a small round conference table.

The chief spoke first. "Your father was a helluva cop. I never got to work with him, but everyone who did respects him. A lot of the state-police detectives want to tell us locals how to do our jobs but not Bart Neumann."

I felt proud, with a tinge of regret that I knew so little of my father's working life. "Thanks, Chief. That's nice to hear."

"He's a cop's cop. But you didn't come here to talk about your old man. What can I do for you?"

"First, I should tell you where I fit into the Tocks Island Dam project. I'm the US Army Corps of Engineers project director, responsible for coordinating the dam construction. I hire the contractors, try to keep things moving, manage the budget, and act as liaison with local communities."

The chief sat back in his chair. "Did you manage the land purchases?"

"Yes. Well, not directly. We have a separate department that handles that. But they report to me."

"Have they told you about their hard-nosed tactics?"

I felt defensive. "Well...they don't involve me in their day-to-day activities, but I am aware that there are sometimes disagreements associated with land values."

"That's putting it mildly." The chief leaned forward and focused his eyes intently on mine. "Look, Jack, I mean no disrespect, but a lot of folks were forced to sell land they wanted to keep, and most of them don't think they got a fair price."

"I understand some people get hurt in the short term, but I think the dam will improve flood control and be a major economic advantage to the area."

Chief Detweiler didn't respond. His stare felt unfriendly.

I tried to sound more accommodating. "Dad told me there is a lot of anger about our land purchases…"

"Most folks up here think they were land grabs, not purchases. A purchase, to me, means you have a willing seller."

"I take your point."

"I know you have a job to do, Jack, but the forced land sales caused economic hardship and broke hearts."

While I was formulating a response, Chief Detweiler spoke again. "Are you responsible for the people squatting on the land you acquired?"

"On paper, I am. The buck is supposed to stop with me. But to date, we've tried all the nice legalities, like eviction notices. The squatters just ignore them."

"Are you aware the squatters have appealed their eviction legally? Got the court to intervene?"

"No, our lawyers never told me that."

"The local judge set a hearing to hear their appeal, but your lawyers never showed up for the hearing, so the judge ruled in their favor. You're going to have to start over to get them off your land."

"I'm sorry. I didn't know. I'll check this out when I get back to my office."

"I'll tell you something off the record."

"Great," I replied. "Looks like there are things happening I'm unaware of."

"I've gotten word from people above my pay grade at the state-police headquarters telling me to stay away from any actions against the squatters. By the way, the squatters call themselves 'settlers.'"

"Really. Who told you to lie off?"

"That I can't say."

"Can't say or rather not say?" I asked.

"The latter," replied the chief.

It was clear he was not going to say more.

I sat quietly. I could hear a typewriter down the hall. A telephone rang in the distance.

"Can I ask a couple of other questions?" I asked.

"Sure," he said; a half smile showed in his eyes.

"It's pretty clear I'm not as informed as I should be. My dad suggested I talk to Emil at the Village Tavern, so I'm going to do that. Is there anyone else you think I should see?"

"Emil knows what's happening around here." He paused. "Why don't you visit the squatters?"

"Really? Do you think they'll talk to me?"

"I'm not sure. But if they do, you might learn something. If they won't, that tells you something too."

"How would I find them?"

The chief opened the top right-hand drawer of his desk, removed a gray metal box filled with index cards, and began going through them. He drew a card out.

"The leader of the squatter bunch is a guy named Will Mead. I don't know if he'll talk to you, but give it a try. Stop at my front desk on your way out, and they'll tell you how to find their locations up off River Road. They like to call their operation 'Cloud Farm.' They may even have a sign out on the road."

"Do you have much contact with them?"

"Tell you the truth, I tell my folks to deflect complaints. We don't have jurisdiction on the federal land, and they make most of their trouble there. Grow marijuana and bring in other drugs—mostly psychedelics, I think. Don't misbehave off the reservation much. They scare the women with their long hair, beards, and raggedy dress, but I can't bust them for that."

"Anyone else I should talk to?"

"Are you aware of the opposition of the environmentalists?"

"I do know about that, yes," I said. "But I don't know any names."

"The best contact for environmental stuff is a woman named Loretta Shuster. I don't have a number for her, but I'm sure she's in the phone book. Husband's name's Paul. She and her family have lived here for generations. Lost some of their land to your dam."

We sat without speaking. The leaves on the oak tree outside the window behind the sheriff's chair shook soundlessly.

I was about to thank the chief for his help, when he spoke. "I can sniff trouble in the air."

I waited. The chief continued, "People are pissed—got a right to be. Outsiders came in and screwed with their lives. Took their land. They're good people—peaceable—but you shouldn't mess with them."

I nodded. "Am I right, most folks in the area are second- and third-generation immigrants from Germany and Eastern European countries?

"That's about right. Lot of Irish too. Irish came to work in the coal mines further upstate. Over the years, a lot of them have moved down here."

I was reflective about the chief's "trouble" comment. "The whole country seems unsettled," I said.

"Damn right," said the chief. "Something evil was unleashed when they killed JFK. Niggers are rioting all over the place—even before they killed Martin Luther King. Now Bobby Kennedy. Didn't like the little son of a bitch, but people loved him."

"And you haven't even mentioned Vietnam."

"Right! One of our kids was killed over there. I went to his funeral in March. Another one was wounded. He's back, but he's had a hard time."

The chief sat quietly for a few moments and then leaned forward. "Enough of the gloom and doom. I've got things to do, and so do you."

I sat in my car outside the chief's office considering my next step. I decided not to go back to Philly that night—wanted to spend some time at the Village Tavern and try to meet with the squatters' leader.

I rented a room at a motel out on Route 309 and called my office and wife to tell them I wouldn't be back for another day. In my room, I lay on the bed and fell asleep—I, a guy who thinks people who take naps don't have stamina, slept for two hours. I woke up groggy, went to the local diner for coffee and a meal, and headed to the Village Tavern.

When I entered the Village, there were about a dozen men scattered along the bar. Two men in the back were shooting darts. I took a seat at the bar about three quarters of the way toward the back. The chatter quieted. *They're checking me out*, I thought. I was glad I'd taken my necktie off and left my suit coat back in the room, but I was still wearing a white shirt. It was the only white shirt in the place.

The bartender put two draft beers in front of customers close to the front door, stopped to chat with them, and then headed toward me. I'd noticed almost all the men were drinking draft beer.

"What can I get you?" the bartender asked.

"I'll have a draft." I put a five-dollar bill on the bar in front of me and then noticed there was no money on the bar in front of other customers. *Things are different up here*, I thought. Down in Philly, the custom is to put money on the bar to pay drink by drink.

The bartender drew me a beer, put it on a coaster, looked down at my money, hesitated, took the money, rung it up, and returned my change.

The chatter along the bar slowly resumed as I sipped my beer. I wondered if the bartender was the Emil I had been referred to and listened for someone to call him by name. He moved efficiently along the bar, filling empty glasses as he went. The customers were clearly regulars. He usually refilled glasses wordlessly. Occasionally, he would stand in front of a customer whose glass was empty, lift the glass, and wait for a gesture from the drinker. Usually a nod or a hand gesture told him whether to refill the glass. No one spoke to me. Occasionally, when I caught someone's eye, they would nod a hello.

I finished my beer and waited. The bartender noticed my empty glass, stopped in front of me, lifted it, and asked, "Another?"

"Yes."

When he placed the full glass in front of me, I asked, "Are you Emil?"

"Yep. That's me."

"My name's Jack Neumann. I can see you're busy now, but I was hoping to talk to you for a few minutes."

"Is it business?" he asked.

"It's not about your business. I'm up from Philly, hoping to learn how folks are reacting to the new dam they're going to build."

He didn't sound unfriendly but asked, "What kinds of things do you want to know?"

I didn't want to be explicit right away, so I answered vaguely, "Well, the dam has multiple purposes: flood control, power generation, recreation. I'm interested in what people think about each of them."

"Who do you work for?"

I noticed the drinkers, near enough to hear our conversation, were listening. "This is unofficial right now."

"I can't talk now, but I get relieved at six. We can talk for a few minutes then."

I looked at my watch; it was twenty-five minutes until six. "Good. I'll hang around till then. Thanks."

Emil moved on to refill more glasses. A little before six, his relief arrived: a big, tough-looking man whose nose suggested he'd been a prizefighter. He immediately went behind the bar and took over bartending. He and Emil exchanged brief hellos. Emil made himself a drink with ginger ale and a generous amount of Canadian whiskey and went to sit in one of the booths along the wall across from the bar; he gestured me to join him.

Emil waited for me to speak. "Thanks for talking to me."

"Sure."

I was uncertain how to start, so we each sipped our drinks. Finally, I spoke.

"I'm with the Army Corps of Engineers, but I work in the Philly office, so I'm not aware of the day-to-day activities with the Tocks Dam project we have going up here."

Emil didn't speak.

"I've been told some of the local people are unhappy about the dam."

"You got that right. I'd use a stronger word than 'unhappy.'"

"What word would you use?"

"Pissed."

I laughed unhappily. "I'm sorry. I don't mean to play down what you say."

Emil was quiet again.

I decided to be more forthright. "Let me tell you where I'm coming from. I'm with the Army Corps of Engineers, and my job is to coordinate construction of the dam, and things are not going well. A lot of the problems come from Washington: construction money is being delayed, and we're behind schedule. There's not much I can do about those problems, and I'm sure folks up here don't care about my problems."

Emil nodded and seemed a little less unfriendly.

"Another problem is my location in downtown Philly almost a hundred miles away from here. I don't have a feel for what's happening locally, so it's only recently I've become aware of some of the things people around here care about."

"Then you understand why I say people are pissed?"

"Only partly. I know our land purchases made some people unhappy."

"Yeah. Quite a few people were cheated."

Again, I was taken aback by his stark assessment and didn't respond right away.

"Look, Jack," he said, "at first I thought the dam was a great idea, figured it would be a net plus for our area and a good thing for my business. Now I'm not sure about the benefits, and I sure as hell don't like the effect your dam has had on our people. A lot of them have been screwed."

I asked a few more questions, but Emil's responses were short and not informative. It was apparent he was not going to be helpful. He drank the last of his drink and said, "I've got to be on my way. Anything else?"

"No, thanks."

Emil got up, waved to the new bartender, and left through the back door.

I didn't sleep well that night—it seemed as if I was half awake and engaged all night in fuzzy arguments with people I didn't recognize. The next morning, I had breakfast at the diner and sat drinking coffee after I ate. I decided I should look at the squatters on Cloud Farm.

I headed north on River Road. The road gave me a view of the Delaware River on my right, except when it curved left and my view of the river was blocked by thick stands of trees. The sun was still low in the sky, but the night chill was gone. A few miles north of Shawnee, I began to see abandoned homes and sagging outbuildings—evidence of our land condemnations. Just after a right curve, with the Delaware River visible in the distance, I saw a farm field with a man struggling behind an old-fashioned wooden plow strapped to a mule. I pulled off to watch. It was slow going for the plower. He stumbled occasionally in the deep furrows. I got out of my car and walked down an incline toward him.

As I approached, the man stopped, took a red handkerchief from his pocket, and mopped his brow. He looked grateful for the interruption.

"I'm glad it's you doing that work, not me."

The man smiled. "I was hoping you were coming to help."

"I'm too old to work that hard. But I'll bet it feels good."

"It feels good—after I'm done."

"I understand. Maybe you can help me, though. I'm looking for Will Mead."

"I know Will," the man responded, offering no more information.

"My name is Jack Neumann. I heard about a commune up this way, and I'm interested in more information."

The man looked suspicious. "I don't know of any communes around here."

"Maybe I'm using the wrong word. Is there a small settlement of people who have moved here recently?"

"Are you with the government? Or the police?"

"No, my wife and I are thinking about buying a plot to build a vacation home. I'm curious about the new community and how it's organized."

"We don't live in a commune. Families have their own places."

"I see," I said. "I see you're getting ready to plant. Do you grow your own food?"

The man seemed to relax a little and mopped his brow again. "We try to grow our own food. It doesn't work one hundred percent."

"Yeah. I can see that would be difficult."

The man was quiet again.

"I hear a lot of this land is owned by the government," I said.

"That's true, including this land I'm plowing. They're going to build a dam. Where we're standing will eventually be under water."

"I heard about that. Would Will know where land is still available?"

"I don't know, but he may know more than I do." The man hesitated and continued, "Okay. I think Will's at home. If you head north, slow down after the second right-hand curve. About two hundred feet beyond that curve, you'll come to a gravel driveway on your right. Go back there and you'll see a two-story red brick house about a quarter mile back. That's Will's house."

I found the gravel driveway less than a mile north and turned in. I didn't see the house immediately, but when I came around a curve, it loomed ahead. As I pulled into the yard, I noticed a woman hanging laundry on a triangle of clothesline anchored around three oak trees. She was short, slender, and barefoot and stopped her work as I parked. She wore a long denim skirt and a plain white blouse.

"Good morning," I said. "I was hoping to talk to Will Mead."

Her long red hair was tied in a ponytail; her pale, freckled face appeared unconcerned. "Around the front. I think he's on the porch."

I walked around the right side of the house, and as I turned the corner at the front, I noticed the land dropped steeply to the river several hundred feet away. I stopped to take in the view. The river's water had assumed the gray color of the clouds that had thickened in the last hour. The river current moved slowly to the right. *The water's flowing south,* I thought. Then I smelled marijuana.

"Can I help you?" A faint swirl of smoke drifted from the man's nose, but he had discarded the joint.

"I hope so. You've got quite a view here."

"You should see it at sunrise when it's not cloudy."

"I'll bet it's beautiful.

Will sat on the porch, six wooden steps up. I asked, "Do you mind if I come up?"

"Help yourself."

I mounted the steep steps, struggling a little at the last one. "My knees don't bend as they used to."

Will nodded but didn't respond.

"My name is Jack Neumann. Am I right that you're Will Mead?"

"That's me." Will offered his hand, and we shook. "Have a seat."

I sat in a low-slung wicker rocking chair; most of its white paint had flaked off. There were a variety of mismatched chairs and a table on the porch that ran the full width of the house. I noticed the wood around the front door, and windows needed repair and paint.

"What can I do for you, Mr. Neumann?" His tone was neutral.

I hesitated but decided to be direct. "I'm going to be frank, Mr. Mead."

Mead interrupted, "Call me Will."

"Okay, Will. A friend of mine works for the Army Corps of Engineers, and I probably don't need to tell you, this Tock's Dam project that's he's got responsibilities for has run into trouble—I think it's the delays that are giving him indigestion." I paused.

Will responded, "I don't know much, except that they want to build a dam, and they've bought up a bunch of land along both

84

sides of the river. I rented this house and acreage while they're doing the preparation work."

"I see. My friend feels like he's in the dark about the local situation. He no longer has folks on the ground to update him. He understands some folks are unhappy about the dam, but he understands too that there are a variety of interests."

"Who is your friend?"

"He works in the Philadelphia office and has to answer to the people in Washington."

"What's his name?"

I hesitated. "I'm talking to you unofficially. I might want to buy a lot up here, build a cabin for my wife and me, and some grandchildren, to use from time to time. I only live an hour southeast of here, in Bucks County."

"If I were you, the first thing I'd do is find out what land doesn't belong to the government."

"Before I look at land options, I'd like to find out about problems in the area. Help my Corps friend out at the same time."

"I'm not sure how I can help."

"I understand there are some folks around here who don't want a dam because they think it will be bad for the environment."

"That's right."

"Is that the way you feel?"

"I'm sympathetic to those concerns, but I've gotten used to living here too. If they build a dam, this place will be under water."

"I understand there's a small community of folks like you."

"Right. We're scattered around some, but this place is a kind of headquarters. We're going to have a cookout here this weekend."

"How many of you are there?"

Will hesitated. "About seventy-five, not including kids. But that number's going up. Some folks leave in the cold weather, come back about now."

"Do the local folks mind your being here?"

Again, Will hesitated. "Some do."

I pressed the point. "What kind of trouble do you have with the locals?"

"Mostly minor. Teenagers come by some weekends. Make a lot of noise. Throw their empty beer bottles out the car windows."

"Anything more serious?"

Will squared his shoulders. "Look, Mr. Neumann. I'm not sure what you're looking for. We're aware some folks resent us and consider us outsiders. So, we try to avoid trouble—keep to ourselves."

I decided not to press Will for details. "Okay. I appreciate the information you've given me. Is there anyone else you think I should talk to?"

"I guess you should check the land records at the courthouse to see what's available."

"Do you know any locals who could round the picture out for me?"

"I can't help you there. Like I said, we keep to ourselves." Will paused. "If you want to talk to someone involved in environmental activities, look up Loretta Shuster."

"Thanks again. Good luck."

On my way back to town, I noted that Will was the second one to refer me to Loretta Shuster.

When I got into Stroudsburg, I found a phone booth and got the telephone number for Paul Shuster from the directory hanging on a chain in the tight enclosure. I dialed the number; a woman answered on the second ring.

"Is this Mrs. Shuster?"

"Speaking."

I decided to drop any subterfuge. "My name is Jack Neumann. I direct the Tocks Dam work for the US Army Corps of Engineers. I'm in Stroudsburg right now, assessing progress on the dam. You've been identified as someone with an interest in the dam. Do you have a few moments to talk?"

"Yes."

I waited for her to say more, but she was silent. "I understand you have concerns about our dam-building activities. Is that correct?"

"I do. As do many others in the area."

"I would like to meet with you in person to discuss those concerns. Are you free to meet with me for a short time this afternoon?"

Mrs. Shuster was quiet for several seconds. I was about to go on when she responded.

"What is it that you'd like to discuss, Mr. Neumann?"

"I'd like to hear your point of view. I might be able to answer questions or explain what we're doing and why."

"It's a little late for that, Mr. Neumann." There was another silence before she asked, "Can you tell me how the instability in the upper and lower mantles of the earth where the dam is to be built will be stabilized?"

I was stunned and silent now myself. I guessed she was referring to the unfavorable geologist's report. The term "mantle" is a technical one that refers to layers of the earth. But I did not want to engage with Mrs. Shuster on this issue.

I asked, "Are you referring to an old geology report?"

"Yes."

"There are differing opinions about that report's assessment."

"Perhaps I haven't seen the latest report. Are there differing opinions about the instability two hundred feet below the surface?"

I had to stretch for my next response. "There are differing opinions about the effects of the instability."

"Is there a consensus among the experts?"

"I believe so. But a full discussion is difficult on the telephone."

"Do you want to send me technical information in that connection?"

I was on my heels now. Mrs. Shuster rescued me.

"May I make a suggestion?" she asked.

"Of course."

"The Lower Minisink Environmental Defense group will meet the Thursday after next. Would you like to attend that meeting to discuss the geology of the location where the dam is to be built? Perhaps you can send us some of the geologist's evaluation in advance of a meeting?"

I decided on the spot that I did not want to meet with Mrs. Shuster or her group. "That's an interesting idea. I'm not in my office now. I'll check my schedule and get back to you."

The last issue I wanted to air in public was the geology report. I drove home that afternoon, and even though it was not yet five o'clock when I got there, I mixed myself an extra dry martini.

Will Mead

In 1965, I was a new assistant professor of sociology at the City University of New York, enthralled by an idea I'd gotten from my studies of community development: that it was feasible to create a viable and permanent utopian community in the spirit of Henry David Thoreau, incorporating his ideas for living in harmony with the environment as well as his prescriptions for civil disobedience to bring about positive social change.

My Ph.D. dissertation had been a study of attempts to establish utopian communities in the United States. That work had convinced me that, in the right circumstances, I could create a new form of human organization that would mitigate problems of modern society. My dissertation had examined why most attempts to establish utopian communities in the United States failed. Earlier attempts often relied on the vision and competence of a single charismatic leader who lacked the organizational skills needed to sustain communities or who failed to arrange for continuity in leadership when they were gone. Still others collapsed because of defective models or because valid models were never fully implemented. I had the idealistic notion that I knew how to avoid previous mistakes.

I was also eager to escape urban living. New York City's problems with housing, traffic, poverty, poor education, and governance seemed insoluble to me. I felt overstimulated and distracted by living and working there. I'd also become fascinated by the recent book authored by Helen and Scott Nearing, *Living the Good Life.* The Nearings had established an independent community in rural Vermont that sustained itself economically through the production of maple syrup.

One day a student came to my small windowless office at NYU and showed me a classified ad in the *Village Voice* advertising real estate for rent in the Delaware Water Gap area of northeastern Pennsylvania. The following weekend a few of us visited the area and were immediately struck by the potential of all the empty houses and fertile land on both sides of the Delaware River. Before long we signed leases with the Army Corps of Engineers for several parcels, and as soon as the semester ended, I resigned my academic position and moved with my wife and three other families to vacant real estate along the Delaware River north of Stroudsburg.

My wife, Rosemary, and I hadn't married yet, but we'd lived together for three years and had a thirteen-month-old daughter. Adapting to our new life was more difficult than we anticipated— we couldn't simply walk to a store five minutes away for baby food, diapers, or a loaf of bread. But we eventually adapted. Sometimes we worried about the effects of our lifestyle on our daughter, Diana, but we were committed to the project, which we viewed was an important social experiment.

We named our little community "Cloud Farm." We worked hard, planting crops and making our new homes livable. The first winter was especially difficult. We couldn't afford fuel for our heating systems, did not cut enough wood in advance to keep our fireplaces fed. Our first crop was insufficient to feed us.

We improvised: signed up for the new federal food-stamp program, had two of our mothers collect welfare, and found occasional part-time jobs. The women worked long hours, making quilts that we sold at a consignment shop in Delaware Water Gap. After a few months, we couldn't afford to keep paying rent to the government. We planned to resume paying when we could get the money together, but that never happened. Not paying rent was a mistake.

Engaged but exhausted by strenuous work, we were sustained by a strong belief in what we were doing. We had escaped the concrete environment of New York City and imagined we'd found an ideal place to live and were on our way to the establishment of an independent new community where we would be happy and that would serve as a model for others.

But, looking back, I see how I deluded myself that my motivations were purely idealism and social science. Truth was, drugs and sex had more than a little to do with my desire to live free from legal and social conventions. I was a regular marijuana user then, and I'd also used LSD occasionally. I found it difficult to be monogamous as well. Cloud Farm facilitated my drug use and provided opportunities for sex with multiple partners. It was years, though, before I could consciously acknowledge these motives.

For several years, the size of our community grew in the late spring, summer, and early fall when the weather was warmer. Two of the original members of our group were musicians, one of them a guitar player with a great singing voice and a large repertoire of folk songs. Not long after we established our community, a couple of folk musicians from New York got wind of our "gig" and came to join us on a few weekends. After a month or two, they returned one weekend and never left.

We began having Saturday-night music get-togethers. These sessions were our only entertainment in the early days. Within a couple of months, a few locals learned about our Saturday-night music sessions and began attending. These sessions continued for several years and were a rare example of occasions when our community and residents joined together in a positive way.

About a year into our experiment, I decided to look for support outside our little group and found a natural alliance with local environmentalists. They were opposed to the Tocks Island Dam because of the damage it would do to the natural environment. At first, we had an uneasy alliance because some of those folks thought our use of the land was a problem. I finally figured out that the main reason for their animosity was because we had moved into homes that had belonged to their friends and neighbors.

I developed a friendship with Sam Kopco, a lineman for Pocono Electric Company. When we first moved to the area, we arranged for electricity for three homes and paid the monthly bills. But when things got tight financially, we couldn't pay. Further, as our numbers grew, we ran power lines from homes with power to other structures. The power company soon caught up with us and disconnected the power. Sam was the one they sent to turn it off. Periodically, we accumulated enough money to pay our bill and got the power turned on. Sam visited us regularly, sometimes to switch our power off and sometimes to turn it back on. Sam and I got friendly. A few times he ignored the jury-rigged connections from one home to another. Sam became a friend over the years, the only lasting personal relationship that remains from my years in the Minisink.

One Sunday night during the second winter, we had a medical crisis with one of our women and her newborn. She was hemorrhaging, and the baby was having trouble breathing. We located a doctor willing to help but were without electricity. I drove to Sam's cabin at about two in the morning, and he came out in the dark, climbed one of the utility poles, and turned on the electricity. I believe Sam saved two lives that night.

When the doctor had things under control and the community was slumbering again, I invited Sam to share a joint. We sat in my living room, dark and quiet except for the glow and crackle of the fireplace. We sat there until a hint of dawn and a cooling fireplace intruded, quiet for long stretches. Sam told me about Vietnam that night. He told me his story in pieces; I think he had to pause occasionally to gather himself. I could not see his tears but heard them in his voice. It was emotional for me too; for the first time, I saw another aspect of the war—the damage it did to those who did the killing.

I am grateful, still, that I heard Sam's heart that night.

By the second year, we were getting eviction notices from the lawyers at the Army Corps offices in Washington. The first time or two, we got the money together to have the eviction notices withdrawn. But our rent and electric arrears built up, and we never could generate sufficient income to clear the debt and pay monthly bills too. A couple of times, we used the local court to neutralize eviction notices. Once they enforced the eviction notice on one of the properties. We moved out but simply went to another of the abandoned properties temporarily. Within a couple of days, we were back in the evicted property by simply cutting the locks they put on the front and back doors.

For a couple of years, I had the energy and creativity to keep Cloud Farm going. We could sustain ourselves with food and other basic needs with what we grew, food stamps and the welfare checks two of our women got. I enjoyed dueling with the Army Corps of Engineers and the electric company. But eventually I began to understand that we would not last long term and lost my enthusiasm for the enterprise.

Rosemary and I were having trouble too. I understand now the main problem was that I was having sex with another woman in our community—Amanda. She was a former student of mine from NYU, a hippie to her core back then, although I heard she eventually joined the capitalist economy in New York City after getting an MBA from Columbia.

But back then Amanda's rusty brown hair reached her waist. She favored long dresses, didn't wear makeup, and didn't own underwear. She was discreet, but eventually I discovered she'd had sex with virtually every man in the community. I was jealous and couldn't acknowledge how contradictory that was with our stated community norms. But eventually I had to confront my own value conflicts.

Rosemary and I began to argue—about a lot of things: how often to do laundry, who should clean the bathroom, what to have for dinner, when we should begin to school our daughter, and on and on. Then one day, standing in the kitchen, she asked, "Are you having sex with Amanda?"

"Yes, I've been having sex with Amanda occasionally."

"I want you to stop."

"But we agreed," I said.

"I never agreed to that!"

"Everyone who lives at Cloud Farm has to agree to our code."

"I didn't get a copy of the code."

"Okay, I'll find a copy for you." I began feeling uneasy on top of my anger. We didn't have a written "code."

"Does the code have a process for modification?" Rosemary asked.

"Of course, it does," I said falsely.

"How does it work? Who approves changes to it?"

"It's a group decision."

"Do I get a vote?"

I was squirming now. "Of course, you get a vote." I searched for a way to end our discussion, but Rosemary knew we didn't have a written code.

"I'll expect to see the code tomorrow," she said.

I didn't respond and left the room.

I stayed away from our house as much as I could for the next few days but eventually swallowed my pride and asked Rosemary if we could talk.

"I'm sorry about the other day. We don't have a written code."

"I know," she said.

I was relieved that she didn't sound angry. "But I thought we agreed how we would live here."

"Well, I grant you I didn't express my opposition to our 'community sex practices.'" She said the last three words bitterly. I started to argue but stopped myself. Rosemary turned and went to look out the kitchen window, her back to me. She was quiet. I sat quietly myself. In a brief minute, she turned to me, tears on both cheeks.

Her anger quieted, she said, "I can't accept it, Will. I thought I might adjust to it over time, but I can't—don't want to. I don't want it for myself, and I can't live in a marriage that is not sexually exclusive."

I couldn't respond. Rosemary waited for my reaction, and when I continued to be silent, she left the room. I heard the door close when she left the house. I went to the kitchen window and watched her walk down the path to the river.

Rosemary and I didn't talk much for a week or so, although I felt we were more sad than angry. Then I asked if we could talk one day when Diana was napping. We sat on the porch, each facing the river.

"I will stop having sex with Amanda."

She was quiet for a moment and then asked, "Do you intend to be monogamous?"

"Yes, I think I can do that."

"Thank you," she said. "I will try harder to make things work here."

At that moment, I had the insight that our marriage had been burdened by Cloud Farm. I was so caught up in the enterprise that I was inattentive to my own family.

"Thank you, Rosemary. I'm going to be a better husband and father."

Our marriage got a lot better, but the pressures of trying to sustain Cloud Farm financially didn't let up, and my own commitment to the enterprise continued to erode. I did not acknowledge my pessimism, even to Rosemary. But after its collapse, she told me she expected it to happen and was relieved when it did.

Sam Kopco

When I was gettin' myself together after 'Nam, I got a lineman's job with Pocono Electric. I maintained the company's power lines and substations in the forested area north of Shawnee. It was a good job for me. My territory covered a large area, but not many people lived there; I could work alone most of the time. I only dealt the public when I was connecting a new customer's electricity or disconnecting the service of customers who didn't pay their bills.

One day, I was headed for Jimmy's Deli in East Stroudsburg in my yellow Pocono Electric truck to get some lunch. As I waited at a traffic light, I saw Mark Kober's red pickup take a left turn out of a side street onto Main Street going back toward Stroudsburg. I decided to follow him, made a quick U-turn at the light, and trailed him. In the center of town Mark turned left, drove back a block and pulled into a parking lot. I followed and parked in the space right next to him.

I didn't know what I was going to do when I got out and walked to Mark's pickup. I stood just behind the driver's door where he couldn't see me. Through the window, I saw him going through papers in a file on his lap. He took some papers from the file, opened the driver's door, and got out. He was startled to see me standing there.

"How're you doing, Mark?" My voice sounded strange—high-pitched and loud.

Mark looked confused.

"Nice day, huh?" My voice was still loud but not so shrill.

He tried to walk past me, but I moved sideways to block him. He stopped before bumping into me, turned to his left, and tried to walk on. I moved in front of him again.

"What're you doing?" He looked confused and scared. My adrenaline was pumping.

"Just bein' friendly," I responded. My voice was low and aggressive now—my jaw clenched.

Mark stepped back. I stepped forward and bumped him, chest to chest, forcing him up against the door of his truck. He was really scared now—looked side to side for a way past me.

"What the hell is this about?" he shouted. The papers he was holding fluttered to the ground.

I grabbed the front of Mark's shirt at the collar with my left hand and raised my clenched right fist. Mark leaned back. I leaned forward, but then, thank God, I got hold of myself and didn't punch him. I lowered my right arm, let go of his shirt, and, without another word, turned and went back to my truck.

Mark shouted after me, "Who the hell do you think you are? You won't get away with this."

I turned to see him straighten his shirt and take a step toward me. I started to go back but thought better of it, got into my truck, backed out of the parking spot, and drove away. It wasn't a minute until I knew I'd made a big mistake.

Later that afternoon, I was connecting power at a new subdivision up by Milford, when my truck radio crackled with a call from my boss. "Sam, finish what you're doing and come to the office."

I knew the reason but asked, "What's up?"

"Just come into the office as soon as you can. This afternoon!"

The meeting with my boss didn't go well. He was a good guy, a little rough around the edges, but I knew his kindness firsthand. He'd hired me knowing I was still struggling with Vietnam and gave me a territory where I could work alone most of the time. He'd bring me into his office sometimes, and we'd just talk. But I knew this wasn't going to be another friendly chat.

The police chief had called him. My boss had convinced the chief not to pick me up—to let him get my side of the story. I hated that I'd put him in an awkward spot, but I couldn't figure out how to tell my boss why I threatened Mark without telling him about Holly. So, I'm sure I seemed like a nut. My boss was still pissed when I left that meeting. He gave me a three-day suspension and told me to think about things and come see him first thing in the morning of the fourth day. But when I left the meeting that day, I was more worried about Holly than my job.

I called Holly at work.

"County commissioners' office."

"Hi, babe." I didn't know how to start.

"Hello, Sam." She waited for me to speak.

"Can I see you after work?" My voice sounded strange to me again.

"Is something wrong?"

"No—well, I have to tell you about something."

"What is it?"

"It's better if we talk in person."

"Now you have me worried, Sam."

"It's not bad. I mean…it's complicated."

Holly was quiet.

"I had a run-in with Mark."

"Run-in! What do you mean 'run-in'?"

"Well…I was going to punch him, but I didn't."

"Where? How?"

"Just a little while ago." I didn't know what to say next.

Holly sighed heavily. "I have a PTA meeting tonight. But I can meet you for a half hour."

"Great…good." As soon as she agreed to see me, I started worrying about what I would say and what she would do.

"I don't like the sound of this, Sam. How about you meet me at the ARoma at five fifteen?"

"Fine…I'll be there."

She hung up without saying good-bye.

Holly pulled up beside my pickup and joined me in the cab. She didn't greet me. "Tell me happened."

"Well," I said, struggling to explain without sounding crazy. "When I saw him, I got really pissed."

"Where did you see him?"

"He was coming over two oh nine."

"He was in his car?"

"Yeah. Right. No, he was in his pickup goin' toward Strouds-burg."

"And you followed him?"

"I was goin' to get some lunch. But, yeah, I followed him into town." I had trouble continuing.

"Okay. Then what! Don't make me drag every word out of you, Sam. Tell me what happened."

"Well. Mark parked, and I parked beside him." I stopped again and then blurted, "I was going to punch him, but I didn't."

"I'm still not getting the picture, Sam. Did you talk to him? Did he talk to you?"

"Well, no. We didn't really talk. I grabbed him by the shirt, but I didn't hit him."

"Just out of the blue? You got out of your truck and grabbed Mark. What did he say to you?"

"I don't remember. Maybe, 'You won't get away with this'!"

She stared at me; I was afraid to look at her. Then she laughed.

"That was really dumb, Sam!" She looked worried, laughed, and washed that look away. "I can see the look on Mark's face. He hates physical confrontation. Did you notice if he peed his pants?"

I finally looked at her—hopefully. "I don't think so. I didn't see a puddle." I tried to smile but couldn't.

"Oh, Sam…Sam." She sounded less angry but serious. "This is a problem."

We were quiet, and I was gloomy again.

Holly spoke finally. "I've been thinking I should check the county land records. Look for some evidence." She looked at her wristwatch. "Remember I told you I thought that Mark's father doctored the records for some land transfers?"

"I remember."

"I should check. See if I'm right. Document what I find. It could come in handy if things get uglier."

My mood brightened. "That's a great idea."

But Holly was serious again. "I'm not happy about this, Sam."

"No."

"I don't trust Mark, or his father. They might try to make something of this."

"You mean about me threatening Mark?"

"That's what I mean." Holly was pissed again. "They'll try to connect you and me."

"They don't know about us."

"No. I don't think they do either. But Mark is no dummy. You can bet he'll be keeping an eye out."

I was about to say something, when Holly said decisively, "We'll have to lie low. Not get together for a while."

"But—" I couldn't finish my objection.

"I'm sorry, Sam. I just can't take the risk."

I was quiet and turned away to look out the driver's-side window.

"Sam. Look at me, Sam."

I turned, embarrassed by the tears rolling down my cheeks. "I'll be alone again."

"Oh, Sam." She took my hand. "It's not forever. Just till I get through the divorce."

"Can't we just be real careful?" I pleaded.

"We've been careful, Sam. It's too risky. I don't want them to have any reason to make me out the villain. Make things uglier than they already are."

"It's my fault, isn't it?"

Holly's voice was soft. "Threatening Mark doesn't help, but it's the Kobers. They're the real problem; they're a ruthless bunch."

"I should've punched the son of a bitch. Really kicked his ass."

Holly smiled, continuing to hold my hand. "When this is all over, I'll hold your coat while you do."

I started to tell Holly about the police chief and my work suspension but decided to keep those parts to myself.

I woke up anxious on the first day of my suspension. Drinking my coffee, I thought about what I'd do without work for five straight days—the suspension and the weekend. I knew I shouldn't start drinkin' and didn't feel like hiking, fishing, or canoeing. I'd started thinking about deer hunting. The last time I'd tried was when I was still in rehab after 'Nam; it didn't work out. I was still weak physically. When I got out into the woods and walked only a half mile, I was exhausted. My rifle felt heavy. I walked and rested, walked and rested, over and over. Didn't bother lookin' for deer. It was discouraging.

I like to hunt alone. I enjoy the evening after the hunt with a bunch of guys, drinkin', laughin', and maybe playin' cards, but I have my own way during the hunt. I go out to where I'm going to hunt beforehand and walk the land—pick out several spots where I'm going to sit and wait. If I can manage it, I'll do that two or three times, but that's usually not possible. Grandpop Pete taught me how to find the signs where the deer graze and move around. I'm good at keeping these spots in my brain so I can find them when I come back.

When I bought my land, I thought I'd find a place where I would build a tree stand. I already had plans for four-by-six-feet wooden stand with walls to shelter me from the wind. It would be big enough for two hunters, I thought, for when I had a son or grandson. You could buy the deer-stand kit with or without a roof, and I'd decided I go without a roof; it cost $200 more with the roof, and I figured I could always add a roof later.

I decided to build a tree stand during my suspension. I had a second cup of coffee, ate a bowl of cornflakes, got dressed, and started walking my land. It was cloudy and cool, but within ten minutes, I was sweating. My land is hillier than it looks. I shed my light jacket and tied it around my waist. A year or so earlier, during one of my walks, I'd seen a spot that I thought would be good for a deer stand. It was just inside my property line on the north. I found the spot right away. There was a small meadow just outside my property line. It looked as though someone had cut the trees down years ago, maybe planning to build something there. There was a narrow, overgrown path leading to the clear spot in the forest on the far side of the meadow.

I walked north looking for a suitable tree for the stand. The forest consisted mainly of red oak and poplar with dogwoods, and a few evergreens scattered throughout. The land had been timbered in the distant past because the trees were mature, I figured sixty-five to seventy years old.

I didn't want the stand to be oriented east because the glare of the morning sun might hinder my vision. I found an ideal tree, a red oak with two almost parallel limbs for the base of the stand, about twelve feet from the ground. The location would allow clear shots from three sides. The tree was a little further from the clearing than I'd hoped, so my shot might be difficult, but I had a pretty good scope for my hunting rifle. And, if necessary, I'd buy a better scope.

I went back to my cabin and called several hunting-supply stores. The only one that had the deer stand I wanted was over in Nicholson. It was about seventy miles away, an hour and a half. I decided to go get the deer stand that day so I could start work the next morning. I didn't get back until after five, but I was ready to begin work in the morning.

I got an early start. It took a couple of hours just to get the building material and my tools to the site. Then, I discovered I couldn't build the base by myself. I needed someone to pass the lumber up to me in the tree canopy and stabilize things while I nailed the floorboards in place. I went to the high-school guidance counselor's office and got the names and phone numbers of a couple of seniors who might be interested in earning a quick twenty-five dollars after school. That doesn't sound like much money today, but it was generous back then. It delayed me until the next day, though, when I picked my helper up after school. I forgot his name, but he was a big kid—a tackle on the football team. Once we got to the deer-stand site, though, we had the base built in two hours. But I had already used two full days.

It only took another day and a half to finish the whole project. Then I realized it would be nice to have something to sit on while I waited for deer, so I built two stools that let you sit at the slits in the wall when you took your shot. That took another day, but I was happy with how things turned out. All I had to do now was to make sure my rifle and ammunition were in order, and I was ready for deer season. Felt certain I'd get a deer this year.

Another good thing was that while I was busy building my deer stand, most of the time, I didn't worry about my job or Holly. But the night before I was scheduled to go back to work, I got nervous, didn't sleep well that night. I needn't have worried, though.

When I met with my boss after my suspension, I told him I was mad at Mark Kober and his father because they were makin' money from forcing people off their land. I told him I'd thought about it and realized I had to keep my feelings about the land grabs separate from my job. I could tell my boss was still a little worried, but he let me go back to work.

I missed being with Holly, but we talked on the phone, and I helped her get information about Leo Kober's land deals. They wouldn't let her search the land records, but I could. As part of my job, sometimes I had to check who owned certain land parcels in my territory and what easements applied. So, when Holly wanted to find out about a land transaction involving Mr. Kober, I could do it. I knew how to search the land records, so when I went to the office, I didn't have to ask for help, and they weren't suspicious about me searching through the records.

We found instances where the assessed tax value of some land was bumped up a lot shortly after the Kobers bought it. This information helped to make a case against them, but it was a couple of years before that happened. And when Holly got laid off and got a job in Philly, I thought I'd lost her for good.

Partly just to distract myself, I scheduled a couple of days off during the second week of deer season to try my luck with the deer stand. I was up in the tree with a thermos full of hot coffee, two bananas, and a couple of breakfast bars while it was still dark. The waning moon was hidden behind clouds, so the dark was almost black. The woods were quiet and damp, warmer than usual. I heard rustling in the tree above and figured I had woken a squirrel's nest as I settled in. The nest quieted when I stopped moving around.

I sat on the floor of the stand facing east and watched the sky. I dozed and opened my eyes every few minutes to look for a hint of daybreak. It seemed an hour before I saw a hint of white in the sky. I waited until it brightened a bit and then moved quietly to one of the stools I'd built. I rested the barrel of my rifle in the slit of the tree stand, the stock leaned on my right shoulder. The ground below sloped slightly west to east. I heard the forest begin to wake up. I expected the deer would approach grazing from the north-west and sat facing that direction.

I was dozing again when something aroused me. There was nothing in my sight line to the northwest. I stayed motionless, closed my eyes, and concentrated my hearing. I heard faint sounds and wondered if I was hearing rodents on the ground. I moved slowly and deliberately to the right. There they were, coming directly toward me—a small group of doe and juvenile deer. But no buck. I moved closer to the slit so that I had a fuller view. There he was: a six-point buck. He sensed me looking, raised his head, and slowly scanned his field of vision. He was so close that I saw his nose twitching. He did not look up. His slenderness and taut muscles suggested youth. I stayed motionless. He finally lowered his head and began grazing again, moving directly toward my perch. I did not like this narrow shot. In half a minute, he was directly below me.

I remained still as the small herd moved below me. I waited a few minutes and then moved to the opposite wall of my enclosure. The deer had spread out as they moved away from me, but the buck continued in an almost straight line so that my view was of his white tail and rack. That too was not a shot I wanted to take. Soon, they were out of range, hardly visible through the trees. I waited another hour, but there were no more deer that day.

The next morning, I was back. The sky was cloudless, so there was a hint of daybreak before it arrived. I did not doze this day as I waited. They came from due north and seemed to move more quickly this morning; the young buck seemed in a hurry. They passed directly under my deer stand, and I waited a minute before moving to the other side. Again, I saw the buck's tail and antlers and had decided I'd try this shot, try to hit him in the back where his neck and shoulders met. But then he stopped and turned to look back; I think he heard my movement. I quickly adjusted my aim and fired. He went down right away. I watched to see if he got up again; I've heard this sometimes happens. But I saw no movement.

I climbed down and approached the fallen buck slowly. I saw his chest heave with a breath. When I stood beside him, it seemed as if he had been stretching his neck to look up when he was hit. I bent to look at his face when his eye moved. I stepped back quickly, caught my foot on a root, and fell backward, my upper back thumping the ground. I scrambled to my feet. The buck was still. I watched for breathing and saw none. But I was shaken, felt no excitement about my kill. I was stunned by my response; I think it was regret. I started to leave but found a boulder and sat.

I wanted to walk away. The thought of dressing the deer meant I would be faced with my kill while I skinned and dismembered him. I didn't think I could do it, not that I didn't know how. I had helped Grandpop dress a deer several times. I didn't want to face the reality of my kill, slice into the deer's body repeatedly during the dressing process. That would make it impossible to deny what I'd done. But the thought of leaving the carcass to be torn apart by scavengers and infested by maggots seemed too great a desecration.

I drug the buck toward my cabin until I found a spot with a couple of dead logs on the ground that would allow me to raise the carcass while I worked on it. I walked to my cabin, got my grandfather's dressing knife, lined my wheelbarrow with newspaper, retrieved a shovel, and went back to work on the carcass.

I forced myself into a detached state of mind as I cut and sliced so that I was hardly conscious of what I was doing. The zombie in me took that buck apart. When I finished, I dug a hole, pushed the head and entrails into it, and covered them.

Back at my cabin, I washed the meat and refrigerated it. Exhausted, I lay down and slept for three hours. When I woke up, I called Will Mead and asked if he wanted the venison. He was delighted. They were often short of meat in their diet at Cloud Farm. I took the meat to Will, stopped at the liquor store on the way home, and bought a bottle of bourbon. I drank half of that bottle as I cleaned the inside of my refrigerator with water and bleach. Then I finished the rest of the bourbon and slept until noon the following day. I don't remember going to bed.

When I woke up, yesterday was already a distant memory. I rarely think of that episode and never hunted again. Another Vietnam scar, I think.

Holly

The day after Sam threatened Mark, I called my lawyer and told him to hurry things along. I'd been refusing to concede anything in the negotiations over child support and the division of assets, mostly because I thought I'd need every dollar I could get but also because I was tired of giving in to Mark. I decided it was time to move on and told my lawyer I'd be more flexible in the division of assets but to try to hold the line on the amount of support Mark paid for Rachel.

I also decided to move down to Philly. Ever since adolescence I'd fantasized about the excitement of living in the "big city." I thought New York City might be overwhelming, but Philly seemed like it might be just right. For the previous few years, I'd paid attention to happenings in Philadelphia, especially its cultural and entertainment opportunities. The city has a rich history and lots of museums and entertainment venues. Broadway plays often ran in the city as the last stop before opening in New York. I'd never seen a professional sports event, and the city had football, baseball, basketball, and hockey franchises. I could picture Rachel and I sitting in Veteran's Stadium with thousands of other people to watch the Phillies play.

I had a cousin several years older than me who moved to Philly right after high school. Sandy came back home at Christmas and would describe her life down there; it fascinated me. She didn't even own a car but could go everywhere she wanted using public transportation. She lived in South Philly with two other girls. She was a sports nut too and could get on the subway and, in ten minutes, be at the city's sports complex. She'd go down there without a ticket a couple of hours before game time and look for someone who had an extra ticket. Usually she bought a ticket for a cheap price, and often it was for a good seat. Occasionally, someone would simply give her a ticket. If she couldn't find a ticket and really wanted to see the game, she waited until halftime or late in a baseball game and could simply walk into the stadium and find a seat. Philly had just gotten a National Hockey League franchise, and she really liked those games. It sounded exciting. I'd never seen a hockey game and thought it would be fun.

I'd called Sandy to get some advice about where to live. She told me since Rachel would be going to school, I'd be smart *not* to live in South Philly and recommended I live in a close north or west suburb where it was safer, there was still public transportation into the city and the schools were better. If you lived outside the city limits too, you didn't have to pay the city's payroll tax, which was about 5 percent I think. I'd wondered why Sandy was so knowledgeable about "family" considerations. Turns out she was dating a divorced guy with a couple of kids and was thinking about getting married. She did marry that guy and wasn't going down to the South Philly sports complex to scratch for tickets after Rachel and

I moved there. Her advice about where to live was spot-on, though. It took forty-five minutes to get back and forth to work on public transportation, but Rachel's school was terrific, and I liked living outside the city where there were lots of trees and people planted colorful shrubs and plants in their yards, even if the yard was tiny.

I started buying the Philadelphia Sunday newspapers at the newsstand in Stroudsburg and went through the "help wanted" sections. At first, I was overwhelmed by the number of jobs. But when I studied the classified ads carefully and made some telephone calls, I began to identify the jobs I might realistically be able to get. In those days, you didn't need a college degree to get a good job.

I didn't tell anybody about my plan to move, not even Mom. I wasn't ready to deal with her resistance, and I'd already seen how upset Sam would get at the possibility. Also, I thought Mark would try to prevent any move that took me out of his control orbit. He'd probably use Rachel as his excuse, even though he didn't use half of his visitation opportunities.

Before I was "laid off" from the commissioners' office, I'd begun to search through the land-transfer records and found some transactions between the Army Corps of Engineers and Leo Kober that were suspicious. The price paid to Leo by the Corps was much higher than his purchase price and far higher than the amounts paid to other landowners who were forced to sell. I had a hunch how Leo Kober got these higher prices. The tax-assessment values of the properties he bought went up by about 50 percent soon after he took title. I didn't know how he pulled that off exactly, but the higher tax value helped explain why he got paid so much.

After I was forced out of my job, things got rough financially. I moved back with my parents, hoping it would just be for a short time. I expected my divorce would go through in a few months and I'd have money to tide Rachel and me over while I got an apartment and job in Philadelphia, but Mark put the brakes on. My lawyer couldn't get Mark's lawyer to move things along. It became clear that Mark would continue to make things difficult.

I had a support order from the court for Rachel. It wasn't much money—about forty dollars a week, I recall—but back then it allowed me to pay part of the grocery bill for my mom and buy personal things for Rachel and me. There was always a delay of several days before I got the support money each week. Mark paid the money to the court, and they sent it to me. But Mark started playing games. He'd fail to pay for a while, and when I complained, the court would get in touch with him, and he'd send a check. He'd pay on time for a few weeks and stop again. There were times when I didn't get support money for an entire month.

I couldn't find an office job in Stroudsburg, so I started waitressing. The money was good, but the hours were not, especially because I had to work during homework time for Rachel most days. This was important for me. My parents didn't help with my homework when I was a kid, and I remember being jealous of my friend Nancy in elementary school because her mom or dad always helped her. I'd vowed to help my children. My mother helped Rachel when I wasn't there, but I was sad not to do it myself.

It was hard for Sam and me to get together. My mom knew about Sam, and she was okay with it, but she didn't want Dad to know. I understood; my father was a sweet man, but he was very traditional. I hated the sneaking around, though.

My parents were lifesavers, but I was unhappy living with them. I had gotten used to my independence, and Rachel and I didn't have any privacy. I couldn't afford my own place, and even if we moved, it would be complicated to arrange care for Rachel. I got madder by the day.

I'd always planned to tell the authorities about Leo Kober's land shenanigans but wanted to wait until my divorce from Mark was final. But with all the ugliness, there didn't seem to be a good reason to wait, and I hoped it might even hurry things along. So, I went to see our local police chief. He was the father of a boy I went to elementary school with. I called the chief's office one day and told his secretary I had some "city-hall business" to talk about. She tried her hardest to get the details but finally agreed to let me talk to him. If I'd told her, half the town would know about it by the next morning.

The next day at lunchtime, I went to the chief's office. I was nervous, had never done anything like this. The chief had a scary reputation among young people too, although I wasn't sure why. He looked stern when I sat across the desk from me, though, and waited for me to speak.

"I work in the commissioners' office."

The chief nodded but was silent.

"I think there are illegal things going on with the dam."

I paused. The chief's body tensed and lifted a little, but he didn't say anything.

"Commissioner Kober gets paid too much for his land."

I started to continue, but the chief got up and walked around me to close his office door. I waited until he sat again. Now he sat forward, his hands folded.

"You know about the dam, right?"

"What about the dam?"

"Well, it's about the land exchanges with the government."

The chief nodded, but I saw a frown around his eyes. "Go on," he said.

"You know the government forced a lot of people to sell their land cheap."

The chief barely nodded; I didn't want to say Leo Kober's name.

"But somebody got a high price for their land."

The chief opened the top center drawer of his desk and got a lined yellow pad. He smiled. "I'm going to make some notes about our conversation."

His smile was forced. It didn't reassure me at all. I wished I hadn't come but couldn't figure how to leave.

"Who got high prices?"

"One of the county commissioners."

His voice was harder now. "Which one?"

"Leo Kober."

He made a note on the pad, but I had the feeling he knew who even before I told him.

"How do you know that?"

There's no going back now, I thought. But my mind raced for a way to avoid details. "He was paid more than the county land records said."

"The land records don't tell how much land will sell for."

"No. But when you look at how much the land is assessed for taxes, you can figure a rough market value." At this point, I decided to be vague going forward.

"Tell me more."

"Well, I thought you would check it out. Some land transactions looked fishy to me."

"Those sales were between our citizens and the federal government. I don't have jurisdiction."

I sensed a way out. "Of course! You're right. I hadn't thought of that." That was true; I hadn't considered the legal-jurisdiction issue. "I'll let the federal government worry about it. It's none of my business."

I could tell Chief Detweiler was skeptical about the last point.

"Why did you come here, Holly?"

"Well, a lot folks who were forced out of their homes didn't get enough money. I was hoping they might get more if we could show how other people got a better deal."

The chief looked skeptical. "What would you like me to do?" he asked.

"I guess nothing. Seems like I just wasted your time. I'm sorry."

The chief looked at me with his hard face, his eyes locked onto mine.

"I do think you're right," he said. "About letting the federal government worry about their land transactions."

I looked at my watch. "Well, my lunch hour's about up. I need to get back to work."

"Okay," he said. His eyes still locked onto mine. "If you want to talk further to anyone about this, do let me know. There is a safe and legal way to go about this, and I can help guide you. But I think your idea to let the federal government deal with this is a good one."

He stood up, so I did too. "Thank you, Chief." I couldn't wait to get out of there.

Years later, after Leo Kober's case was adjudicated, the chief's secretary told me I was barely out the door before he called Mr. Kober. Stroudsburg was really a small town in those days.

I was nervous, but I decided I was not going to let it go. But I wasn't sure what to do next. Some of the land exchanges were out in the county outside town or over in New Jersey. It was clear to me now that the fraud was against the federal government, not local interests. The closest FBI office was in Philly, so I called them. They didn't seem interested either. Finally, the third or fourth time I called, they referred me to the US prosecutor in Scranton. That was less than an hour away, so I drove over there my next day off. That got things moving.

I talked to a good-looking young lawyer, Jeb Rooney. In fact, I was a little distracted by his sexiness at first; I had trouble paying attention to what he was telling me. Later, I found out he was married with three kids, so I squelched my fantasies.

We talked for a couple of hours at that first meeting. He gave me a list of questions and information I should collect. Many of the details he wanted came from the county's land records; he asked me to go to land records at the courthouse to collect it.

When he paused, I asked, "Can you protect me from them?"

He hesitated and then looked me in the eye. "Do you think you'll be in danger?"

"I might be."

"If you have serious concerns, maybe you should forgo doing what we've discussed. Because, honestly, I can't offer you protection. Now if you are threatened or attacked, I might be able to help you after an occurrence."

"But not before," I noted.

"I'm afraid not."

I sat thinking for a minute and then decided. "I want to go ahead."

"Good. You're doing a good thing—a courageous thing—and I will advise you how to stay safe as best I can."

When I went to the land-records office at the courthouse the first time, I knew for sure that the Kobers were on to me. I was acquainted with the lady in land records, but she wouldn't let me look in the files; she told me they were reorganizing them. But I could look right over her shoulders and see others working with the files. She rolled her eyes to let me know she was being forced to keep me away from the records.

I called Jeb. He told me to write down what happened, sign and date it, and have a witness too. He told me to go back and try again and, if the same thing happened, make another record. I went to the records office three times and made a written record each time they refused to let me get any information. I sent all this information—Jeb called it "evidence"—to his office in Scranton. But it was months before anything happened.

I called Jeb every couple of weeks. For a while he told me he was still gathering evidence. Then for a while, he was coordinating with New Jersey officials. Eventually, he was waiting for instructions from Washington. I know now there was a lot going on I didn't know about, but it was frustrating. The FBI was collecting evidence; the lawyers at the Army Corps of Engineers were involved; some inspector general from an agency I can't recall was doing something else.

I got more nervous by the day. I think my divorce lawyer was nervous too. Nothing was happening, and he seemed to want to get off the phone whenever I called him.

Then the scary stuff started to happen.

I came out after work one night, and all four of the tires on my car were flat. The cook stayed with me until the tow car came. Three of the tires had long slashes in them, so they were not repairable. My automobile-insurance company told me I wasn't covered for vandalism. Mom and Dad came to the rescue again and bought me a new set of tires. Then I made sure I had insurance that covered vandalism.

Another time, a beat-up pickup forced me off the road on the way home after work. It was late, eleven or so, and I had to walk back to the restaurant to use the pay phone. In the dark, I wondered if that guy in the pickup might come back. To make it worse, when I called the cops, they took a report but never did anything as far as I know.

When Mark came to pick Rachel up for a visit or when he dropped her off, he'd threaten me. "You should stop talking to strangers," he said a couple of times. Or, "You shouldn't be going out by yourself at night."

I started to have my dad with me whenever I had to have a contact with Mark. It was scary but funny too. Dad would stick a loaded pistol in his waistband and make sure Mark could see it. The first time Mark's eyes got big as saucers. If you knew my dad, you'd understand how out of character it was; he was not an aggressive guy. Eventually he got so mad at what was happening to me that some newfound aggression started to show. At times, I was afraid he might shoot Mark, but there was something reassuring about it too.

Finally came the indictment of Leo Kober and "coconspirators." I didn't even know some of the people listed as coconspirators or really what that might mean until I saw the big headline in the local paper. Local TV news covered everything that happened, such as when Leo Kober refused to talk to a local reporter. A couple of months later, the newspaper ran a series of articles about the land deals—compared the prices Leo Kober got with what others got. They found some fishy deals I wasn't aware of. They indicted the woman who headed the tax assessor's office too. Apparently, she helped Leo Kober raise the assessed value of his properties.

I thought, *Well, finally!* I'll stop being scared, and folks will rally to me. But that didn't happen. Stroudsburg was still a small town, and a lot of folks viewed me as a troublemaker. The threats stopped, but I still felt uncomfortable. At the grocery store, I'd see people cutting their eyes at me, and at work I noticed my tips shrank. The divorce kept dragging on. I wanted to get out of Stroudsburg so bad that I thought about just leaving town and taking my chances, but I knew that wouldn't be good for Rachel, and underneath it all, I'm not a big risk taker.

Mom and Dad got me a new divorce lawyer, and he got things moving. It still took about six months, but finally I had the divorce decree and a nice hunk of money in the bank—enough to tide Rachel and me over for a year or so in Philly in case I couldn't find a job.

Before moving I decided to test the job market in Philly, hoped it might help me decide where I should live down there. I set up three interviews in downtown. The first was in a shabby looking building on Race Street down by the river. When I saw the location, I canceled my interview. The other two were okay. One was in a department store where I would work in a large open office area with about twenty other women. I think they would have hired me, but I couldn't see myself working comfortably with other desks all around me. The third was in a lawyer's office, but they wanted someone who could type a hundred words a minute. That wasn't for me either.

I decided to try one more time before moving and was in the process of lining up another day or two of interviews when I got a call from Jeb in the Scranton prosecutor's office. He had a colleague who worked in a large downtown Philly law firm who was interested in hiring someone to interview clients and witnesses for cases his firm was litigating. I didn't know what litigating was until I looked it up in the dictionary and asked my lawyer to explain what it meant in practice. It sounded interesting, so I went down for an interview.

The interview went well. They wanted someone who had good "people skills" and said they could train me in the legal knowledge I would need. Two days after the interview, they called and offered me a job paying more than I was making at the commissioners' office. I sensed my good looks helped, but that turned out to be okay; nobody harassed me at work.

I was a bit unsteady the first month or two after Rachel and I moved. All of a sudden, I was a lone adult living in a big city, a new school system, needed someone to care for Rachel after school, uncertain where to shop and how to get around. They put a lot on my plate at work right away, and half the time, I wasn't sure what I was doing. My head spun. When I got home from work, I was exhausted.

But after a while, things settled down, and Rachel, thank God, was happy as a clam. She did well in school, made new friends, and never complained—even in the beginning when I didn't have the energy to do things with her.

Sam was a mess, though, and I couldn't give him much attention. I tried to explain, but he didn't get it. One time on the phone, I got angry and told him to "stop whining and grow up." We didn't talk for a while after that.

After a few months, things settled down, and I began to feel as though I had control of my life. I learned how to use the public transportation, and we used it a lot. We started visiting some of the area's attractions. Rachel loved the Franklin Institute downtown, and we went there several times. They had science games kids could play. I loved the art museum, only a couple of blocks from the Franklin Institute and a small Rodin-sculpture museum close by too. There was a huge mall only five miles from where we lived; sometimes we went there and just walked around looking in the stores.

I got a different picture of what was happening in the country. The *Pocono Record*, the daily paper in Stroudsburg, in those days emphasized local news, and I rarely watched the six o'clock news before I moved. In Philly, I started to read the *Philadelphia Inquirer* on my way to and from work and began to learn about the happenings in the country and world. I was amazed at the turmoil—especially about Vietnam. There were a bunch of colleges and universities in and around the city, and there seemed to be an antiwar demonstration at one of them every day. The women's movement got more attention down there. And there was more open talk about sex at the office than I was used to. One day at lunch with several other women, the sex talk got specific, including details of oral sex. I know my face was red that day. All that took some getting used to, but after a while, I lost my small-town-girl attitudes.

In those days, many of the shows headed to Broadway played in Philadelphia first. I took Rachel to see two of them. One was a musical whose name I can't recall, and the other was a drama.

We went to a Phillies-St. Louis Cardinals baseball game one Sunday afternoon. She really loved that. A boy with a baseball glove a few rows in front of us caught a home-run ball. On the way back home that night, Rachel pestered me about getting a base-ball glove. She knew exactly where to get one—at a sports-goods store over in the mall. She went on and on about it for days, so we finally went to the mall and bought one. She took it to a couple of Phillies games but never had a chance to catch a ball with it. The glove stayed on top of her bureau for years, though. Years later when she played softball in high school, she tried to use it, but it was too small. But the first glove still sat on her bureau. She did leave it at home when she went to college, though.

I dated. There were several teenagers in my apartment complex, so I could usually find a babysitter when I was asked out. I went out with one of the young lawyers from the firm for several months. He was cool and took me to nice places, and his apartment was only about ten minutes from mine. But he started talking about marriage and got possessive. He started to remind me of Mark Kober, so I stopped seeing him.

I was happier dating a couple of different men and learned how to juggle things. I even had a couple of one-night stands, but one of these guys had weird sex ideas. I wondered if I was simply naïve, so I talked to one of the girls at the office who I knew would keep it to herself. She agreed with me and advised me to stay away from that guy.

I decided quickly one-night stands left me feeling uncomfortable, so I decided they were not for me.

All but one of the guys I dated were nice guys. He was so shy that he could hardly talk. Sitting across from him at dinner was painful, and I drank so much wine that his face was fuzzy by the end of the meal. Then, when he brought me home, he got pushy and wanted to come in for a "nightcap." I had to push the apartment door closed against him. Then he banged on the door. I finally told him I was calling the cops. He left then.

When Sam came to visit, I let him stay with us and sleep on the couch. Rachel liked Sam, and I got more and more comfortable with him, especially after he stopped being so needy and sad. When he quit asking me to come back to Stroudsburg, and waited for me to invite him to visit, we started to have a more comfortable relationship, and my strong feelings for him grew. Sex with Sam has always been great. It was awkward to have sex with Rachel home, but most weekends when he visited, I'd find a way to have Rachel play with a friend for a while, or I'd have a babysitter take her to the movies.

Sam kept me up-to-date on the Tocks Island Dam happenings when he telephoned and visited. I was happy to be away from the turmoil. It seemed everyone up there was grumpy, even though daily life kept on as it always had. The schools and churches kept doing their thing. The men went hunting on schedule. Most of all, the beauty and majesty of the mountains and valley held steady.

I'm glad I spent those years in Philly, but I never quite lost the feeling of being just a little out of my comfort zone in the big city. There was an unspoken commitment between Sam and me. I'd stopped dating, and Sam began to look for a job around Philly. I was feeling like I might want to go back to the Minisink Valley but hadn't said so out loud. Then Sam got a job offer, a good one, with the Philadelphia Electric Company working out in a rural area north of the city. That brought things to a head.

I called Sam one night. "Do you really want to move down here?" I asked.

Sam, in character, was quiet.

I got tired waiting for him to answer. "Do you want some time to think about it?"

"I'd rather stay here...I think."

At that moment, I had the strong realization that Sam would be uncomfortable leaving the Minisink and would not adjust easily—maybe not at all.

"When do you have to decide about the PE job?"

"By the end of next week."

"I think this is a big deal, Sam. Give it more thought, and call me next week."

I began considering what I wanted and what my options were. I had a couple of long talks with an older woman at work who I'd recently become friendly with. Beth was a grandmother but didn't look or act like one. I think she was still in her forties. I sensed she would understand and give good advice, and I was right.

Beth had lived a more tumultuous life that I thought. Her parents divorced when she was a teenager, and she had been divorced. Like me, her first marriage had been brief, but she didn't have any children from that marriage. She was in her midtwenties when she remarried and was still married to that man; they'd had a girl and a boy together. The girl was in her last year of college; the son had enlisted in the navy right out of high school and planned to go to college when his enlistment ended.

Beth was a great listener, and I talked to her at length. I was torn. I liked living in Philly, but it was lonely at times. Rachel was happy enough and doing well in class, but I wasn't crazy about her school situation. There were some rough sections of our school district, and there seemed to be a lot of kids struggling academically. I'd heard too that the junior and senior high schools were riddled with drugs and gangs. I couldn't afford to move to a better school district. The better ones where public transportation was available were too expensive for me, and if I moved further out in the suburbs, I didn't know of a place with good public transportation.

I missed Sam too. I liked being with him, and truth was, he needed me. I worried about his lack of ambition and his emotional dependence, but on the other hand, I was sure he'd be faithful, and I knew he would be fierce about protecting me.

Beth helped me sort this out. She had a saying I hadn't heard before or since: *Nothing's forever. Circumstances change, and we change.* I didn't get how this applied to me right away but finally understood: if things didn't work out, I could change my situation again.

But I wasn't going back to the Minisink without a decent job—one that was interesting and might have a future. I liked the legal work I did, but there were not many jobs like what I did up there.

I could earn a little less money because I could live more economically back home, and I knew my parents would help with Rachel, so my babysitting costs would be less. I was sure I would feel a certain security back home too. As interesting as it was living in Philly, I always felt a slight unease living there. People were simply not as open. Not that they were unfriendly, just a little reserved. I guess there is *no place like home.*

One day at work, I called Jeb and told him I was thinking about coming back and wondered if he knew about any law-firm jobs. He didn't but promised to let me know if something came up. I didn't say anything to Sam, Rachel, or my parents.

About six weeks later, Jeb called. Another law firm in Scranton was looking for a legal assistant. I took an afternoon off and went to interview. They weren't looking for someone to do exactly what I was doing in Philly, but they liked the experience and insight I'd gained at my current job. And they knew the firm I worked for. I was unaware, but not surprised, that my Philly firm had an excellent reputation. I left the interview feeling good. Sure enough, they called a week later and offered me the job. The salary was the same, and the benefits weren't quite as good, but I was satisfied it would be okay. It was a forty-five-minute commute to Scranton, but that was about the same as my Philly commute. I asked for a few days to think about it and called Sam that night.

After the pleasantries, I took a deep breath. "I'm thinking about coming back to the Minisink."

There was no hesitation. "Really. I'd love that. I'd rather not leave."

I never heard Sam sound more excited. I told him about the job but wanted to have a serious conversation too. We had a heart-to-heart; we've only had a few of those in all our years together. This was our first. I wasn't ready to marry or to cohabitate. Remember this was the early 1970s. Living with a man you weren't married to, especially in Stroudsburg, wasn't acceptable.

So I accepted the job, found a nice two-bedroom apartment in East Stroudsburg, and one weekend Sam came down and moved us. His pickup was loaded. I followed him all the way back home to watch for anything that might fall off the truck.

I left Philly feeling good. They had a farewell party for me at work—gave me a beautiful framed picture of boathouse row along the Schuylkill River downtown with the individual rowing club buildings decorated with Christmas lights. It's a lovely and iconic Philly scene. People drive up and down the Schuylkill Expressway at night during the holidays just to look at it. As soon as Sam and I bought our house, it was the first picture we hung on the living-room wall.

Even more wonderful than the picture were the cards and notes people gave me. I rarely cry, and never in public, but I did as I read those notes at my farewell party. I never fully understood the way folks related to each other in Philly and, I guess, maybe in big cities generally. I always felt a certain distance, even with people I knew pretty well that I didn't feel back home. But their notes to me were sweet and loving.

I'd brought Rachel to my farewell party. She often asked questions about my job and office that I felt I hadn't answered very well. She was curious about what I did and the people I worked with, so I thought her curiosity might be satisfied by seeing the office and meeting the people I worked with. She loved it. My coworkers made a fuss over her, and she had an extra helping of cake and ice cream. She was chattering about her experience driving home, and at one point, she stopped and said, "I liked those people, Mom; I could tell they really liked you a lot!"

That started me crying again.

Back in the Minisink, I discovered that I was still viewed as a Judas by some people. I wanted my move back to the Minisink Valley to be permanent. I hoped never to leave again, so I decided I should act like I belonged—be active in the PTA at Rachel's school and look for other opportunities to get involved. I wasn't back a week before I had a hint that we wouldn't be welcomed back with open arms. Rachel came home from school one day in her first week and told me a girl in her class had told her, "Your mom is a troublemaker."

Rachel didn't seem upset; she was confused. "I don't know what she meant, Mom."

I hadn't said anything to Rachel about the land-fraud case. She understood that her father and I were divorced, but I hadn't told her about any of the unpleasantness with our financial and other disagreements. Rachel had been great amid all the changes: going to live with my parents, moving to Philly, and coming back to Stroudsburg. She'd acclimated to new circumstances and made new friends. Her only complaint had been about the things she kept in her bedroom. In our move to my parents' home, I'd packed her stuffed animals and knickknacks in a couple of boxes that I didn't unpack immediately.

Putting her to bed on the second night at my parents' house, she was tearful, and I couldn't get her to explain what was the matter. I don't think she knew herself. I had a hunch and went to get her favorite stuffed animal, a rabbit with long ears and pink eyes. The rabbit had originally been a bright white but had become a dull gray from being with Rachel constantly. It had been a challenge to stop her from taking the rabbit with her when she went to play outside.

As soon as Rachel had her rabbit—his name was Cloney for reasons I never understood—she was comforted and was asleep within minutes. After that, the first thing I did when we moved was unpack Rachel's bedroom stuff.

The last thing I wanted to happen was for Rachel to have trouble being accepted at school, so I went to see her teacher. She was great. We planned for me to come to school one day, and Rachel and I described our time in Philadelphia, emphasizing we were natives of the Valley and coming back to live permanently. It worked! Rachel became a celebrity of sorts, having lived in the "big city." Her descriptions of the Franklin Institute especially impressed the other children. They had a large section on an upper floor that was dedicated to hands-on play experiments for kids to carry out.

I could head off trouble for Rachel but not for myself. Within a month of returning my car was vandalized—a broken windshield in the supermarket parking lot. I didn't go out at night by myself much, and when I did, I worried. I asked Sam to accompany me, which I hated, but he loved.

I joined the Minisink Valley Environmental Defense group. That was positive. I found people who were supportive of me personally and a group that was doing work that I thought was important. Loretta Shuster became a mentor. Eventually, I told her about the federal prosecutor's activities. Late in the process, I helped coordinate the Minisink Environmental Defense's antidam activities with the land-fraud case.

Sam and I could get together privately at his cabin almost weekly. We needed and savored these intimate interludes. Our sex was hungry; the nakedness and music refreshed our souls, and it was an escape from all that was roiling the Valley.

Finally, they set a trial date for Leo Kober and his codefendants. I feared the constant publicity about the case would result in increased attention to me and my role, but I was wrong. It seemed to have the opposite effect. Folks started to focus on Leo Kober and the hated land grabs. The trial wasn't going to start for a few months, so I didn't have to worry about testifying for a while. I dreaded that. Jeb had told me that I was a key witness and would be cross-examined *vigorously*—that was the word he used.

Then as it looked like there would be a trial, I had to spend time with Jeb preparing to be a witness and then reserve time in my schedule for a trial of uncertain length. This happened twice.

As it turned out, there was no trial. Leo pled guilty to one felony and several misdemeanors just before the trial was to begin. Was I relieved! I was unhappy that Mr. Kober didn't go to prison, but he got a huge fine, five years' probation, and had to resign his county commissioner's seat. He soon disappeared from public view. He stayed in Stroudsburg, but I rarely heard about him. I saw his obituary in the paper ten or twelve years ago. It didn't say anything about his conviction.

Loretta Shuster

About six months after we formed Lower Minisink Environmental Defense, folks started to pay attention. Fred Dugan and I used a strategy he devised, which was to constantly call attention to us and our cause. Fred called at least one person every day—federal and state representatives, Army Corps of Engineers offices, newspapers, the Department of Interior, any public or private person or agency—that he thought might have an interest in the dam, pro or con.

After President Johnson signed the Wild and Scenic Rivers Act protecting the Delaware River, Fred was in touch with someone at the Interior Department at least once a week. After Fred talked to someone, usually on the telephone, I would send a follow-up letter to remind them again of our interests. I was at my typewriter writing these letters many nights after everyone in my family had gone to bed.

Those years were difficult. My two children were still in high school, and even though Paul helped a lot, my parents often needed attention. Dad started drinking heavily after he lost his farm, but it took a while to figure this out. My mother was a lovely person—kind, supportive, and dependable—but she was very dependent on Dad; she never learned to drive, for example. After they moved to East Stroudsburg, Mother would call to complain that Dad was sleeping too much or spending too much time dozing in front of the television. For a while I'd simply try to comfort her. Sometimes I'd drive over to their house and visit for a while. We began to take them to church with us on Sundays, and we'd all go out to brunch afterward.

I thought Dad was simply depressed and needed time to adjust to his new situation, but after a few months, things didn't improve; in fact, they got worse. Then one morning I got a call from the police. They said Dad had been driving erratically and implied he was drunk. They hadn't given him a sobriety test but simply requested me to come pick him up at the police station in Stroudsburg. I was shocked, convinced the police must be mistaken about his condition. I'd never seen Dad take more than a drink or two. When he played cards with his friends every week, I'd heard him brag that he switched to Coke after two drinks while most of his card-playing buddies continued drinking. He attributed his financial success at poker to his sobriety and his friend's excessive risk taking from drinking too much.

Even when I got to the police station and saw my father's condition, I thought he must have had a stroke or some other medical problem. But when we got into my car, I smelled the alcohol.

"Dad, have you been drinking?"

He was silent, so I turned off the engine, and we sat without speaking for several minutes.

"I'm sorry, Loretta. I've been trying to cut back."

I was still stunned. Finally, I asked, "How much are you drinking?"

He sighed heavily. "I don't know…a lot."

We were silent again.

"How about if I make an appointment for you with Dr. Fitzmaurice?"

He sighed again. "That would be fine." His tone and demeanor reeked helplessness.

I burst into tears and was unable to control my sobs for some time. When I regained my composure, I looked across at Dad; he was crying quietly. I saw a tear fall off his chin. It almost broke my heart.

I reached across and took his calloused hand. "Let's go home."

Dad tried to stop drinking. Dr. Fitzmaurice prescribed a tranquillizer initially, but this medication was as disabling as the alcohol. He slept too many hours and could not motivate himself to leave his chair in front of the television. He stopped taking the tranquillizers and soon was drinking again. He started to spend the afternoon hours at the Village Tavern. Twice I got a call from Emil to come pick him up. I got another call from the police to come get him at the police headquarters. This time they told me that if it happened again, they would charge him with drink-driving.

Dad had a couple of periods when he didn't drink for a month or two, but the dry spells didn't last. Finally, there was that horrible day when Mother called, hysterical. By the time I got to their house, the emergency medical people had him on a stretcher, totally wrapped in a white sheet. I tried to get them to remove the sheet so that I could verify he was not breathing, but they convinced me it was futile, and Mother needed my attention. I next saw him in his coffin.

The period after Dad died was the worst of my life. I could hardly keep up. My own grief turned quickly to anger, but Mother got depressed and stopped taking care of herself and her house. Dad's estate was not complicated, but it took more than a year to sell their house. We built an addition onto our house, and Mother came to live with us. Our older child was getting ready for college, and I took her to visit several campuses. She wanted to stay in Pennsylvania, but each campus visit took a couple of days. Paul helped, but he had a lot going on at work too.

I tried to continue the environmental defense work, but it was difficult. Fewer of the contacts Fred made got follow-up letters, and I didn't begin new initiatives. My determination to stop the dam intensified, though. Dad's death stoked me.

While all this was going on, Sam Kopco, with Holly's help, built a record of Leo Kober's land transactions. Sam identified transfers between Leo Kober's land-development company and the Army Corps of Engineers where the amount paid to Kober was suspiciously high. It seemed the high prices were justified by the county's tax-assessment amount, but we hadn't figured out how this increase was justified or who was responsible.

For a long time, we weren't sure how the questionable land transactions would help our cause. But Leo Kober was a strong supporter of dam construction, and as a county commissioner, he had a platform to exercise influence. For a while we didn't do anything with the incriminating information. Fred Dugan had a good sense about leverage, honed during his career when he often had to navigate between the bank he worked for and government regulators in New York.

When momentum seemed to be growing in favor of dam construction, we decided to send a letter to the local prosecutor asking him to investigate the land transfers. The federal prosecutors over in Scranton tried to persuade us not to do this, but they weren't doing anything to discourage dam construction, so we went ahead. As it developed, having simultaneous local and federal action underway brought things to a head quicker.

In the letter to the local prosecutor, we listed several transactions as "suspicious" and provided financial details. The numbers were impressive. There were big gaps between the amounts paid for properties by Timber Development and the amount they received when they sold it to the government, usually less than a year after they bought the land. We sent copies of the letter to a bunch of others: the local newspaper, the Army Corps of Engineers inspector general, and the state attorney generals for Pennsylvania and New Jersey. Then we waited. At about this time, we also became aware that Holly was talking to the federal prosecutor in Scranton.

Nothing happened right away at the newspapers we'd contacted, so Fred visited the editor of the Pocono Gazette. At first, the editor denied knowing anything about the letter but eventually acknowledged that he and the newspaper's ownership had decided to wait until there was some legal action before they did a story. Fred convinced then to print a Letter to the Editor from our organization containing essentially the same information that was in the original letter. It appeared in the newspaper a couple of days later. It helped that there was a federal case going on too. The locals didn't want to appear to be naïve or complicit.

We began to talk publicly about the letter and distribute copies. We pinned copies to bulletin boards around town and made sure the bars and restaurants got copies. It didn't take long. Within a month, folks were talking about the "land fraud." There was a large receptive audience of folks around the Valley that had a sense of injustice about the shabby treatment of their neighbors.

I believe this was the single-most effective thing we did to stop dam construction. Leo Kober's conviction did not come for a couple of years, but we could feel things starting to move in our direction. Looking back, I understand the larger picture. The Vietnam War itself was not going well, opposition to the war was intense, civil rights demonstrations and urban riots broke out across the country, and political figures were assassinated and attacked. Lots of people who were inclined to trust their country's leadership began to question it. Tocks Island Dam was already in its death spiral, but Watergate and President Nixon's resignation killed any possibility that local folks were going to allow the dam to be built.

Our relief that the dam would not be built was short-lived, though. Fred began to pick up hints that a group of commercial developers were attempting to get approvals for a "Vacation Village" in the area. We gradually discovered this "village" was to include one hundred single-family homes, one hundred chalets, a one-hundred-room hotel, a marina with 150 boat slips, and a boat dealership with a repair-and-service operation. And, of course, this development would require new roads and other supporting infrastructure.

We were horrified. This development would be worse than the dam. So even though we won the initial battle, we had to crank up Environmental Defense activities again. When the commercial developers saw how well organized we were, they dropped their plans.

Sam Kopco

Igot home from work one day and found a notice from the post office that they had a package for me. I left work a little early the next day and picked it up. It was a small brown box from the army, wrapped in thick tape and stamped "personal" several times in big red letters.

I drove home wondering what the army was sending to me years after my discharge. It took my pocketknife and a pair of scissors to get through the taping and into the box. When I looked inside, it took my breath away. At the bottom of the box were my dog tags, the knife I carried in Vietnam, the small billfold I used when we were on patrol in the jungle, and my tan army-issued handkerchief lying in the bottom. I lifted the handkerchief, found it stiff, and realized it was stained with my own dried blood.

I'd seen enough and started to close the box but noticed a small white envelope standing on end against the side of the box. I opened the envelope and found my army ID, the ID of the Viet Cong sniper I had killed about ten days before I was wounded, and the picture I thought I had purged from my mind. I was back there again.

We were moving cautiously through thick undergrowth outside a tiny Vietnamese hamlet the Viet Cong used for an operating base. A sniper was threatening our progress, so we took cover in a stand of trees. We couldn't spot the sniper up in the canopy, so Vince Jay, from Pittsburgh, enticed the sniper to fire at a helmet raised on top of his M16 while I watched for a muzzle flash. I didn't see a flash, but I did see an upper branch of a large tree move about a hundred feet straight ahead. I aimed my M16 at the spot, concentrated my vision, and, within a few seconds, detected another slight movement. I fired. The sniper broke tree limbs as he fell; it seemed cartoonish—the man's arms and legs swimming above his torso as he fell. I charged as he thumped to the ground, planning a shot to the head if he wasn't dead already.

My bullet had struck the man in the throat an inch above his breast-bone. As I raised my rifle, the man's terrified eyes stopped me. His eyes engaged mine; his mouth opened and closed as if he was trying to speak. I lowered my rifle—a concession, I later came to understand, that opened the door to the feelings that still haunted me. In a minute, his eyes clouded over, and his convulsing mouth quieted.

The protocol for dealing with dead enemy soldiers called for a search of the man's person, recovery of items found, and giving the material to the company's intelligence officer. This sniper had little on his person: extra ammunition, a small canteen of water, a few dry biscuits wrapped in a soiled cloth, and a small clear plastic billfold with a picture ID card. When I turned the billfold over, I was engaged by a picture of a dark-haired, smiling, pretty, young Vietnamese woman. A pouty little girl who looked to be five or six years old leaned against the woman's left side. I'm

144

not sure why, but I put the packet in my pocket. I looked at the picture frequently.

From then on, I was a reluctant warrior. The anger I used to feel toward the enemy turned to sadness and confusion. The only thing that I was sure about was that I didn't want to be where I was, doin' what I was doin'. Eventually, I understood the enemy soldier was like me. He was doing his job, would likely rather be home with his wife and daughter. He was a reluctant warrior too.

It wasn't until years later that I fixed the blame on those in Washington and Hanoi and other places. But guilt about killin' that little girl's father lingered just beneath the surface.

I collapsed the box and put it and the bloody handkerchief in the trash, but I couldn't trash the other contents. I put my dog tags, knife, IDs, and the picture in the bottom drawer of my chest of drawers where I kept stuff I couldn't throw away.

I was nervous, my breathing shallow; a feeling I hadn't had for a while. I'd stopped keeping beer at home, so I headed for the Village Tavern. The after-work crowd was in place, filling about half the seats. I went to my preferred spot at the far end and took the last stool next to the wall. Several acquaintances at the bar waved or nodded. Emil was busy at the other end.

One of the things I enjoyed about the Village was that, if you were a regular, you didn't put your money on the bar and pay drink by drink; you paid when you left or when Emil was moving from behind the bar to a seat in front of it after he was relieved by the night man.

Emil's memory was amazing. He didn't keep a written tally but knew exactly how much each drinker owed, and we had learned not to question his math. If you kept track, and some guys did, you always found the bill was a little less than you owed—the "discount for regulars," Emil called it. It was about 5 percent. If you argued with Emil about your bill, you had to pay drink by drink.

Emil set a mug of beer on a coaster in front of me. "For my favorite electric man." I drank that first beer quickly, and Emil refilled my glass. The second one went down fast too, but I still had butterflies in my stomach. When Emil filled my empty glass this time, he hesitated in front of me; his antenna was sensitive.

"I'm okay," I said. "But I'm real thirsty today."

He nodded, moved off, and made sure to keep up with the pace of my drinking that day.

When Emil was relieved by the night man, he made himself a drink and came to sit beside me. We didn't talk much, and when he finished his drink, he asked, "I'm going to get something to eat at the diner. Have you eaten yet?"

"No."

"Want to join me?"

I didn't feel hungry, but I was grateful for the invitation. "I'd like that."

The diner was crowded, warm, and heavy with the smell of food; I imagined mashed potatoes covered in thick brown gravy. My appetite woke up. I followed Emil to a small booth just outside the swinging doors to the kitchen. Emil sat, but I hesitated because there was a pile of newspapers and a gray metal box on the table. Emil gestured me to sit across from him. I sat, and almost immediately Dot, the waitress, came to gather the newspapers and metal box. She cradled them on her left arm and wiped the table with her right. She looked at me and asked, "Coffee?"

"Yes."

Waitresses rushed back and forth to the kitchen. Emil and I sat quietly until Dot delivered two coffees and put menus on the table. Emil added a half teaspoon of sugar to his coffee and looked across at me while he stirred. I looked around the diner. I saw only one empty booth and a few empty stools at the counter.

"I eat here three to four times a week," Emil said. "My wife doesn't like to cook, and she's not real good at it anyway."

I smiled. "I'll bet she's good at other things."

"She is. Don't know what I'd do without her."

I studied the menu, but Emil didn't look at his.

Dot stopped at our booth. "Do you have turkey tonight?" Emil asked.

"Yes; with gravy?"

"Right. String beans too."

Dot waited for me to speak. My nose had been accurate. One of the day's specials was chopped steak with mashed potatoes. "I'll have the chopped-steak special."

"What vegetable?"

"How about corn?"

"Creamed or kernel?"

"Kernel."

Dot scooped up the menus and pushed through the door to the kitchen. Almost immediately, she came back and put a basket of rolls on our table.

Emil sipped his coffee, put the cup down, and, in a conspiratorial voice, said, "I know it's none of my business, Sam, but are you gettin' laid?" His face was serious, and he looked a little embarrassed.

I smiled. "I have been, M. But maybe not enough."

"I don't want to poke around your private life, Sam, but sometimes you seem lonely."

"I know. I don't join in much. I've never been real social, and it's gotten worse since 'Nam."

"Are you okay, though? I mean, can I do anything? Do you need to talk to anybody?"

Emil's face was still serious. I realized, *He's worried about me.* I was moved; tears popped into my eyes. "Thank you, M. I guess I worry people who know about me and 'Nam."

"I hope you know you have friends who will help."

"I do, M."

Then, I found myself telling M about the package and the picture. "I got a box from the army today. It had some stuff in it that took me back."

Emil waited.

"I killed this sniper. Shot him out of a tree. He had a picture of his family in his pocket. He had a little girl." I had trouble continuing.

Emil was quiet.

I took a deep breath. "I wonder about the little girl. Before then, I didn't give a shit. The gooks were nasty motherfuckers trying to kill me and my buddies. When I understood the sniper I killed had a little girl, the killing got different. I didn't want to do it anymore. But I had to…"

"Back up, Sam. How do you know the guy had a little girl?"

"He had a picture in his pocket."

148

"And the army just sent it to you? After all this time?"

"Yeah. The package had everything that I was carrying when I was wounded. My pocketknife, ID...I guess someone stored the stuff, and recently, someone else found it and sent it to me."

Emil sat quietly.

"I couldn't get it out of my mind that I'd killed that little girl's dad."

Emil spoke. "I was in the army in the big one—World War II." It was my turn to listen.

"I was lucky. I was in the rear, in supply. A paper pusher. I could hear the artillery, and occasionally I'd have to drive some officer up to the front. But then I'd turn around and come back to the rear. The worst of it for me was the casualties. I'd try not to look at them, but sometimes I couldn't avoid the wounds and body bags. In the winter, some of the bodies were frozen stiff—looked like twisted mannequins for a surplus army-supply store."

"That's bad," I said. "Head and stomach wounds are the worst. And getting it in the balls."

"Sometimes they'd assign a guy who'd had an emotional breakdown to work with me for a while—they called it 'battle fatigue' back then. Didn't send them to the hospital. Just waited until they got themselves together a little and sent them back to the front. Some of those guys were damaged beyond repair, couldn't fight anymore. One poor son of a bitch had his buddy's severed head land in his lap."

Emil hesitated and looked across at me. "I felt guilty bein' in the rear. I had it so easy compared to those other guys. I was ordering soup while they were gettin' killed and wounded. It was dumb luck. I believe I was assigned to supply only because I'd worked as

149

an office clerk part time when I was in high school. I felt guilty, but I didn't volunteer for combat either."

Emil looked and sounded different—the table between us not like the bar that usually separated us.

He spoke again. "We both did what we were told to do. I was lucky, got to do something easy. You had to do something hard."

Dot brought our meals. We ate in silence.

We skipped dessert but had another cup of coffee.

Emil asked, "You're involved with the environmental group that's trying to stop the dam, aren't you?"

"Yeah. Others are doing most of the work, though. I give them information that I come across from my job." I didn't tell him about Leo Kober's swindles.

"I had a conversation with a guy from the Army Corps of Engineers the other day. I think he's part of management."

"Really? Did you find anything new?"

"Not really. Seemed that he was looking for information about the local folks' feelings about the dam. I didn't tell him much."

"I'll let Loretta Shuster know."

When I went home after dinner with Emil that night, I went to bed early and slept dreamless through the night.

I had been thinking about Coach Sweeney's suggestion that I come to the high school's wrestling practice and decided to give it a try, but I was uncomfortable about putting myself in the spotlight in front of the young wrestlers, afraid they'd want to talk about Vietnam. The more I thought about it, the more I was determined that after I got that package from the army, I needed to face my discomfort and expose myself more.

My high-school wrestling years had been great; I was happy and confident. I didn't mind the hard work at practice or the hours running and lifting weights. I got good, so I almost always won my matches. I loved the camaraderie of being a part of the team. Coach Sweeney was an important influence too. He knew how to be tough with me without making me feel bad.

Recently, I'd been following the wrestling team in the local newspaper and noticed East Stroudsburg High had a dual match coming up with Mahanoy High School. I wrapped up work early one day and went to watch.

I wasn't ready for the effect of being in the gym that day. When I stopped at the door of the gym to pay three dollars for my ticket, the noise and the smell took me back. The sound in the gym is hard and shrill, I guess, because it's bouncing off the cinderblock walls and wooden floor. The whistles made me flinch the first time or two. The smell of the place brought me back too. The smell is different, hard to describe—pungent but not unpleasant. There's a hint of sweat in the gym's odor. The only other place that smells a little like our gym with the wrestling mats rolled out is the bowling alley, and that's not real close.

I found a seat about halfway up the stands behind our team's bench. Clusters of wrestlers were scattered around warming one another up, practicing their moves. Coach Sweeney was huddled talking intently with a young man who looked to be in his early twenties—the assistant coach, I assumed. I watched the wrestlers in the lower weight classes warm up. I always felt the low- and mid-range weight classes were the most interesting. Lighter wrestlers had to rely on skill more than strength, although the bigger guys don't agree with that. They say it's just another kind of skill.

A loud whistle made me jump again and started my adrenaline. It was time for the first match. I watched the two wrestlers go onto the mat—105-pounders. I knew right away who was going to win. The East Stroudsburg wrestler walked confidently to the center of the mat; the Mahanoy wrestler's body language looked reluctant. Sure enough, the Stroudsburg wrestler scored a takedown within thirty seconds. The Mahanoy wrestler escaped but was taken down again almost immediately, and before the end of the first round, the Stroudsburg kid got a pin.

The next set of wrestlers had different body types. The Mahanoy wrestler looked thicker, stronger, but the Stroudsburg boy was a couple of inches taller with longer arms and legs. *Strength versus leverage,* I thought as they began to wrestle. These two were evenly matched. Each got a takedown and an escape in the first round. As they grappled during the second round, I realized my body was tense and twisting along with them. I was surprised that the thick-bodied Mahanoy wrestler was as limber as he was. Toward the end of the second round, he began to dominate and almost got a pin. The Stroudsburg wrestler started the third round strong, but he faded after a minute, and the Mahanoy wrestler took advantage and won the match 12–7.

In the breaks between matches and rounds, I watched Coach Sweeney talk intently to his wrestlers, often using his hands on their arms and shoulders to demonstrate his point. It brought me back to my time with him. I remembered his intensity. He'd wrestled in college at Penn State. For me, this intensity, not the techniques or moves he suggested, had the most influence. During a match, I usually left these coaching moments with renewed determination.

Today, I found myself sweating and breathing heavily during the close matches. It took effort to relax my body when a match ended. About halfway through the competition, I looked down and saw Coach staring up at me, hands on his hips. I waved. He nodded and turned back to his next wrestler.

I started to look at the full scene: the opposing team's coach and team. I didn't recognize Mahanoy's coach. He was tall, slender, and young—didn't look like a former wrestler. He had a much different style than Coach Sweeney—more laid-back. The wrestlers on his bench were different than Stroudsburg's kids—less animated. They rooted for their teammates but in a less demonstrative way—*like their coach*, I thought. Their coach wasn't a wrestler, I decided, or he was inexperienced.

I looked around the stands. There were few spectators. This was typical, I recalled; dual meets during the workweek didn't draw many people—mainly friends and family of the wrestlers and a small number of fans interested in the sport. There weren't any cheerleaders for either team. When I wrestled, I didn't mind the low turnout. When we had tournaments with a bunch of teams and later in the season when teams were fighting to win league championships and when individual wrestlers were fighting to move on to state-level competition, the crowds were much bigger. I liked the smaller crowds; it took me a couple of years for me to get used to bigger crowds and the noise. It helped when I learned to tune all that out and concentrate on the action on the mat.

Stroudsburg won the meet, although it was close, and the victory depended on us winning the heavyweight match. Our heavyweight was not skilled, but he dominated his opponent with aggression and won by three points.

I went to the locker room afterward and heard the last couple of minutes of Coach's congratulations speech and his instructions for the next day's practice. He motioned me to accompany him to his office when he finished. I sat across the desk from him.

"Good to see you, Sam. Did you enjoy watching?"

"I did. I sweated along with your guys."

"It doesn't take much to bring the old instincts back."

I chuckled. "I was surprised."

"My offer stands. I could use your help. My one-hundred-sixty-five-pounder is a lot like you were. I think he'd benefit from your coaching."

"I'd like to help, but I don't see myself as a coach. Besides, I don't usually finish work this early."

"Why don't you try it, see how you like it? Could you come one day a week?"

I found myself warming to the idea. "I'll talk to my boss. See if it's okay with him."

I talked to my boss, and we made a deal. I left work two hours early three days a week during wrestling season, and when I had to take care of a power outage or some other problem after regular work hours, I didn't put in for overtime. My boss was old school; he hated payin' overtime.

It took a while to figure out how to fit into Coach Sweeney's practices. I spent a lot of time watching the kids work on their technique. Gradually, I developed an eye for the various wrestlers' strengths and weaknesses, and we figured out a division of labor. I was better at working with wrestlers in the low- and medium-weight categories where technique and quickness were key. When I wres-

154

tled, one of my strengths was quickness. Most of the best wrestlers below 180 pounds have a good instinct for the right move and go for it fast. I discovered ways to improve a guy's quickness. I had some physical drills that helped, but my main emphasis was on concentration. When I wrestled, I got into a zone. My world got smaller and quieter, and I watched my opponent's legs and torso to anticipate his moves as soon as he started to make them. Sometimes I was so focused that I didn't hear the coach shouted instructions during the match. He would get pissed at me for not doing what he said, but usually it was because I didn't hear him. When I was a senior, he trusted my instincts when I was on the mat and didn't shout instructions very often.

Coaching became a big part of my life. I was an assistant coach for about ten years, and when Coach Sweeney retired, I became the head coach and did that for another ten years. When I was head coach, I didn't win any team state championships, but I had several individual wrestlers who won the state title in their weight classes. I developed a reputation for developing sound wrestlers, so college coaches came to recruit my guys. But I'm most proud of helping to develop solid young men and, I believe, saving a few who were headed in the wrong direction. Becoming a good wrestler is as much about commitment, hard work, and character as it is about physical skills.

When I got into my fifties, I noticed my Vietnam emotional scars bothered me less and less. One day I realized my dream about Ace getting blown up hasn't happened for a long time. Occasionally, though, I have a different dream: *I'm wounded and lying under the thick green cover on the ground in the jungle. I can't move or talk. I can hear my platoon moving further and further away; they've forgotten me, and I can't holler to them. I think I will die there.* Then I wake up. It doesn't happen that often, and I can usually calm myself and go back to sleep. I don't think I holler in my sleep anymore either. Holly would tell me if I did.

About twenty-five years ago, my army company started to have reunions. I went to the first one, but I only saw a couple of guys I remembered. My buddy Kirk didn't go. By then, his construction company had grown a lot; he said he was way too busy to attend. Kirk handled the Vietnam memories differently than me. He really resists talking about them. I do too, but he drew a sharp line. He told me once that I was the only one he ever talked to about our time over there.

I went to the first reunion and tried to join in the activities, but it felt phony. I stayed stoned and went to bed early. That weekend is a blur. I didn't go to another reunion for years.

Then Kirk killed himself. It was right after the turn of the century, March 2000. They said his death was accidental—carbon-monoxide poisoning from a defective space heater in his workshop—but as soon as I heard, I knew it wasn't an accident.

I went to see Kirk's wife a couple of months after he died. We didn't talk about the accident or suicide question, but I could tell she thought Kirk had done it himself. She told me how, a few days after he died, she found a note from him at the bottom of her underwear drawer.

"Just like Kirk to leave the note with my underwear," she said.

The note told her to get a metal box from the top shelf at the back of his workshop. She had a hard time holding things together as she told me what she found. I take it there were practical things

such as a will and how to get to his company's records. What was
important to her, though, was a love letter.

"It sounded a lot like a letter he sent to me from Vietnam," she
said. "I saved the 'Nam letter. The one he left for me said some of
the same things. That was really comforting. But I'm till pissed at
the son of a bitch for leaving me."

We laughed and cried at the same time.

A few months after Kirk died, I got a notice about another
reunion. I hadn't gone for years, and it got me thinking. I had
pretty much gotten over killing the sniper—able to see it as a
responsibility, I had to protect me and my fellow soldiers, but there
was something else that I felt ashamed about, something I had
nothing to do with. It was the My Lai Massacre, where a US army
platoon, led by Lieutenant William Calley, slaughtered hundreds
of civilians in the hamlet of My Lai, in South Vietnam. The victims
were mostly women, children, and old men. When things became
public, it was clear that Calley and his men had gone through the
village killing as they went without any threat from the people. I
knew it didn't make sense for me to feel any responsibility for My
Lai, but it still bothered me.

The massacre had occurred in March of 1968 but didn't
become public for a year and a half. When the story did make the
nightly news, there was a lot of controversy, many arguing it never
happened or that the victims were Viet Cong soldiers. Almost right
away, my gut told me "massacre" was probably the right word, and
eventually, Lieutenant Calley was convicted of a bunch of the murders, and other army officers were court-martialed for a cover-up.
Calley got a life sentence but was later pardoned.

I wondered if My Lai was a scar for other vets. It is well known by now that the country treated returning Vietnam veterans badly—I think we got blamed for the failed war and the embarrassment it caused. I believe too that My Lai helped fuel the animosity toward returning Vietnam vets.

I did something I never thought I'd do. I called the VA and made an appointment to see a psychologist. I had to talk myself into keeping the appointment, but I'm glad I did. The guy I saw was cool. He was a vet himself and one of the most laid-back people I've ever met. He had this smile that seemed to sneak onto his lips without his permission, sometimes at times when I didn't see anything humorous in what had been said. His sense of humor was a little off-key. His name was John, which I always thought was too plain a name for him. But he had a big heart, and I got to like him a lot.

John was blunt, didn't beat around the bush. In our first meeting, after he got my personal information, he put his pencil down, leaned back, and said, "How can I help?"

"Well, I'm not sure, but I'll tell you why I'm here. I'm doin' okay, I think, but I have this idea. I guess I should tell you about me first, though, right?"

"Maybe not," he said. "I've reviewed your file, so I'm aware of your service history. I know you had serious wounds, and I have your physical-treatment records. I don't have any indication in your file that you have consulted a psychologist before. Is that correct?"

"Yeah, pretty much."

"Okay, why don't you start then?"

Suddenly, I felt angry. "So I'm supposed to do all the work here."

"No. But it's not complicated. Can you simply describe what motivated you to come here? I can ask a bunch of questions, but it's usually best if you get us started."

"Right. Okay." I took a deep breath. "Maybe I should have come here earlier, but I didn't. After all these years, I think I'm okay mentally." I looked at him, but he didn't say anything, so I went on. "I'm thinking about going to a reunion of my army company. I haven't been for years. I went once, but it was depressing, so I haven't gone back."

"I'm familiar with that group," John responded. "They were involved in some of the heaviest fighting, had a lot of casualties."

"Like I said, I'm okay now. Had nightmares for a long time, but they don't happen much anymore. The first few years after 'Nam were hard. I lived like a hermit and drank like a fish. Had a lot of guilt. A couple of weeks before I was wounded, I shot a sniper; the guy had a picture of his family in his pocket. I felt bad…that bothered me for a long time." I waited again, but John simply nodded.

"I still have the picture, but I haven't looked at it for a long time—don't dream about it anymore. A couple of months ago, my best buddy from 'Nam killed himself." I took a deep breath. "He seemed like he was doing great—married a long time, raised three kids, had a successful construction company."

"What was his name?"

I gave him Kirk's full name and where he lived. John wrote down the information and put his pencil down again.

"That's not why I came, but I guess I wonder if there's something inside me that could make me off myself."

"I'll be able to say whether I think you're a suicide risk after we talk more, but why did you come?"

"It's kinda a long story."

"I've got time."

"Recently, I started thinking about My Lai." John took a deep breath himself but didn't say anything. I went on. "For some reason, the My Lai Massacre got me thinking about my own experience."

My words started to come easier.

"For a long time, I felt guilty about 'Nam—ashamed of killin' that little girl's father, gettin' my pet monkey killed, leavin' my platoon to fight without me after I got wounded, didn't always step up when the fightin' was bad. I shuda done more. I didn't help Kirk either."

My chest hurt.

"Where's the My Lai connection?" John asked.

I tried to organize my thoughts.

"I thought I'd found a way to get rid of my own guilt when I thought about My Lai—maybe that I was no more responsible for what I did over there than I was for My Lai—but that doesn't seem sensible."

John was quiet for a few moments. "So, you're comparing your guilt about what you did or didn't do over there with My Lai?"

"No. Not that exactly. Maybe I shouldn't feel any more guilt about what I did than about My Lai. I wasn't anywhere near My Lai when all those people were killed, but I felt ashamed when I heard about it. It dawned on me that there was no reason for me to feel bad about My Lai or my own killing. I was doing what I was ordered to do."

John leaned forward. "Think about this. How about if we separate your feelings about the victims and your actions?"

"I'm not sure I follow you."

"You felt bad for the little girl and her mother in the picture, right?"

"Right, and the father too—the sniper."

"Okay. And you feel bad about the My Lai victims."

"Right. But I didn't kill them."

"Bingo," John said. "You're feeling compassion, a positive, healthy response. Do you know what empathy is?"

"Yeah, I know what it means." I was a little insulted, even though I was a little fuzzy about the meaning.

"That's what you're feeling about the My Lai victims and the sniper and his family. It's separate from any responsibility you have for their deaths."

I sat thinking about what he said.

"Do you believe killing is sometimes justified, like in war?" he asked.

"Yeah, at least I used to. I did when I was in 'Nam. But now, I'm not so sure. The pricks in Washington told a lot of lies about the war. To us and to the folks at home."

John smiled. "Now you're exposing some contradictions we should talk about, but we're out of time for today. I have people waiting. Can you come back at the same time next week?"

"Sure."

"Good. I think you're doing well. Are you going to be okay until we talk again?"

"Sure. What's another week?"

I met with John five times. It was some of the best time I ever spent on anything. I got a lot freer. I rarely think of Vietnam anymore. And something interesting came out of it too.

During the last two sessions, we talked about having a panel discussion at our reunion later that year. John thought it might be helpful to use My Lai and the discussions he and I had had as a "new way" to talk with other Vietnam vets. He thought it might be helpful to other vets and to me.

My Lai had stirred up a lot of controversy in the country. There were some who thought the whole thing was a myth and others who thought the United States should be brought before some international court for war crimes. And it didn't seem as if there was any agreement about what should be done about those who did the killing and all the army officers who had covered it up. John thought there'd be some vets whose emotional adjustments had been thrown off by all the My Lai talk.

He came to our reunion and gave a two-hour seminar he called "My Lai, Me and Vietnam." He had it on the first afternoon; he said he wanted to do it before the partying got too far along. He asked me to be on the stage with him, but I wasn't up for it. Instead, he brought an army master sergeant who had done two tours over there.

I went to the seminar. It was interesting. He made clear from the beginning that they were not going to discuss the rightness or wrongness of My Lai or the guilt or innocence of anyone. He and the sergeant imitated the discussion I had with John—distinguished the sorrow or sadness about the lost and damaged lives from feelings of personal guilt, shame, and responsibility. They left a lot of time for the vets to ask questions. I watched and listened closely.

A few guys were loud and critical—tried to deny or justify the massacre. A few guys left the seminar early. There were two or three who stayed angry. One interrupted a couple of times with sarcastic comments; he finally left, shouting, "This is bullshit" on his way out. But it helped some of those guys. I could see it on their faces. By the last half hour, the room was quiet and peaceful. There were still differences of opinion but also an "agree to disagree" attitude.

It helped me too. I still had some conflicts within me, but they were quiet. I recognized they might never go away altogether but that I didn't have to keep chewing on them. I was proud too, thought I had contributed something to the other guys at the seminar—maybe even helped John be a better counselor.

Jack Neumann

I had just settled behind my desk when my secretary buzzed. "General McMaster is on the line."

I used my cheerful voice. "Good morning, General."

"Have you heard about a land-fraud investigation up in the Poconos?"

"About the Tocks Dam?"

"Of course! Why else would I be interested?"

"No, General. I haven't heard anything like that."

"You got your head stuck in the sand? Or up your ass?"

"I was just up there last week. I know there's a lot of unhappy people, but I didn't hear anything about land fraud."

"Okay, okay. I got a call from the Justice Department yesterday. The US attorney in Scranton has been investigating for months. Apparently, they think there is enough evidence for an indictment and decided to check with Main Justice before filing the case."

"Come to think of it, General, I did pick up some reluctance to talk to me up there—especially from the local police chief. I could tell he wasn't telling me all he knew."

"An assistant attorney general is coming to brief me tomorrow, so I'll know more then."

"In the meantime, I'll check with our land-acquisitions people to see what they know."

"Don't bother," the general said. "I already called them. They do have their heads up their asses. Or they're holding out on me."

I was beginning to feel threatened—as though I wasn't managing the Tocks Island Dam project well enough. "Okay, shall I wait to hear from you then?"

"Yeah. I'll call you tomorrow after I meet with the Justice Department lawyer." The general hung up without saying good-bye.

I got another call from the general in the early afternoon. "We gotta talk, Jack. Can you hop a train and come down tomorrow morning?"

"Sure. I can take the seven a.m. train and be at your office by eleven."

"Good. You're on my schedule for two hours. Then we'll have lunch."

"Shall I bring anything?" I offered.

"No need."

"Can you tell me a little more? In case I can dig anything up. Or, at least give it some thought."

"Okay, sure. I don't have a plan in mind yet, but I'll tell you what's happened to precipitate my concern. A woman who worked in local government in Stroudsburg has been talking to the US attorney in Scranton about land we bought for the dam where it looks like we paid too much. So far, they don't have evidence that our people were in on a scam, but they're suspicious that one of our guys might be involved. I don't have a name, but you and I need to make a plan."

"Okay. I'll see if I can dig anything up before I come."

After I thought about it for a few minutes, I decided not to make any phone calls before I met with the general. But I did dig out a listing of the land parcels we acquired. They were not much help. There was so much variation in the amounts we paid based on acreage, proximity to the river, and whether there were buildings on the land that I couldn't identify purchases prices that seemed out of line.

I got to the general's office just before eleven the next morning. General McWilliams is a no-nonsense guy. As soon as I was seated across the desk from him, he asked, "Do you know a man from Stroudsburg named Leo Kober?"

While I was racking my brain, the general continued, "He's a county commissioner, owns a land-development company."

"No, General, the name is not familiar."

"The US attorney says he's been selling us land at inflated prices."

"I looked at our records yesterday. They're sketchy, and I couldn't find anything suspicious."

"We may get lucky and find out our people didn't do anything wrong, but I want to be sure."

"What can I do?" I asked.

"I'm not sure yet."

I waited. The general was quiet, sat back in his chair staring down at his desk. Then he spoke. "Can you stay here this afternoon?"

"Sure; I can get a late train back. Stay overnight if needed."

"Okay, here's the deal. I don't think you'll have to stay overnight, but I have our land-acquisitions guy coming over at three. He's bringing records. I'm hoping we can identify some of the transactions that are of interest to the US attorney. Maybe get a sense of whether we have any exposure."

"I'll be happy to help."

I spent some time giving the general a detailed update about the Tocks Island Dam project, and we went to lunch. He relaxed then and told me about some of the things he was dealing with. What got my attention was the likely reduction in funding for Tocks Island Dam. Our congressional oversight committee wanted us to find "economies" so that they could move money elsewhere. The cost of the Vietnam War had created budget problems nationally. The general explained how he was being squeezed to find cost savings and worried that any hint of scandal with the Tocks Island Dam project would give our overseers an excuse to cut the budget. We also discussed how our political support was slipping. Another concern was that the recently elected New Jersey Governor Cahill was having second thoughts about the dam because of infrastructure costs his state would have to pay if the dam was completed. I understood better some of the reasons behind the general's grumpiness about the project. He didn't say so, but I understood if we were unable to keep the Tocks Island Dam project moving due to lack of funds, it would jeopardize the entire thing.

We met with the head of our land-acquisitions division and looked at all the Corps' purchases of Kober Development land. He acknowledged the amounts paid seemed high compared to comparable transactions.

"I talked to our guy who handled most of the deals. He insists he followed our guidelines and used our formula for establishing value. He did acknowledge that he got a couple of free dinners from Leo Kober, and I could discipline him for that, but, frankly, I'd rather not. He one of my best employees, and it's been common practice for our people to accept incidental gratuities like that."

The general spoke. "I don't care about whacking your guy if we're clean otherwise. But here's something I don't think you know. I'm told that after Leo Kober bought land, almost right away, the tax-assessment value of the land increased—usually a lot."

The acquisitions manager looked confused.

The general continued, "Don't we use tax-assessed value to help establish what we'll pay?"

"Ah, I see. That could help account for the high purchase prices."

We were quiet for a minute, processing how the fraud was executed.

The general spoke. "If this holds up, I think we're okay. Do you two agree?"

We each nodded our agreement.

"Good. I feel better about the legal situation. I hope there are no surprises when I talk to the US attorney."

On my way, back to Philly that night, I took stock and concluded the risks to me for mismanagement of the project or fraud were slim or nonexistent. But I thought the likelihood that the dam would ever be built was decreasing, and I was right about that.

Holly

I was only back in the Minisink a couple of months when one of the partners of the law practice where I worked called me to his office. Mr. Farlow wanted to hear more about my experience working for Monroe County. He was especially interested in how and why they fired me. I was nervous—worried that my job at the law firm was at risk. Mr. Farlow noticed my discomfort.

"There's nothing for you to worry about, Holly. We're very happy with your work. The firm is thinking about starting an employment-law section. There's new federal legislation that protects employees from discriminatory treatment by employers. Your treatment by Monroe County may not come under the new law; the legislation focuses on racial and ethnic bias by employers, but if we're going to add this specialty to the practice, we don't want to be hemmed in only to cases covered by the new federal law."

I relaxed. We talked for a while about my Monroe County job and losing it, and he asked me to gather any records I had. I didn't have much. I don't think I ever got a formal notice when they fired me. I began to wonder whether I might be entitled to monetary damages because of why I lost that job.

I didn't hear any more for a while and wondered if they'd decided not to pursue the employment-law specialty. I was about to inquire whether I might have a case against Monroe County, when Mr. Farlow's secretary stopped by my little office to set up an appointment for the next afternoon.

When I went to that meeting, I found Mr. Farlow, one of our young lawyers, and a stenographer who took notes. I must have looked scared again because Mr. Farlow smiled and said, "I assure you, Holly, this is a friendly meeting."

I was nervous, but it was a friendly meeting. Mr. Farlow did most of the talking. The long and short of it was that they thought I had a case against Monroe County for damages and asked my permission to institute legal action against them. They offered to handle the case and to do it for half the fee they usually charged. It wouldn't cost me anything if we lost—a contingency-fee arrangement. They gave me a copy of the agreement and told me to review it and consult anyone I wished. Their only stipulation was that I keep the agreement secret until the legal process was underway. My head was spinning when I left that meeting.

I talked to my dad and Sam, and it seemed like a no-brainer. I didn't plan to ever work for Monroe County again, so I had nothing to lose and a lot to gain. I signed the papers. Mr. Farlow told me it would be a while before anything happened, so I put it out of my mind. That was easy because I had a lot going on. Sam and I had decided to get married, and I had enrolled in night school at East Stroudsburg State. So, with the job, setting up a new household, school, and Rachel, I had trouble keeping up. Then, we decided to have a baby. Seems kinda crazy looking back. But it was the right choice. I wanted to have a child with Sam, and he wanted one too—a boy. Thankfully, we got Sam Jr.

When Sammy was born, I took a semester off from college, but it was still crazy. I didn't take maternity leave from work. The firm was accommodating; they let me do most of my work at home and didn't quibble about the number of hours I worked. I remember being exhausted all the time, though. Sam and Rachel were great helpers. Rachel was something; she wanted to do it all, so we had to limit her. She preferred changing Sammy's diaper to her homework.

Things eased up when Sammy was about eight months old. We found a woman in town to care for Sammy during the day. Sam would drop the baby at her house in the morning, and I'd pick him up on my way home from work. She took care of Sammy during the day until he started first grade. Sometimes on weekends Sammy would ask to go to Miss Prout's house. The nanny's last name was Proud, but he could never manage the *d* sound.

For a year or so, my law firm tried to get a settlement from Monroe County by negotiating with them directly, but eventually, the county dug in their heels. Mr. Farlow thought the advancing fraud case against Leo Kober made them pull back. So, we filled a lawsuit. Then, there were more months of waiting.

In about my third year in night school, I started to enjoy the intellectual part of college. New worlds were opening to me—especially in literature and history. I started to think beyond a bachelor's degree and talked to Mr. Farlow and other attorneys at the law firm about law school. For a while, it seemed unrealistic. But as time passed, Mr. Farlow, who had become a mentor, gave me the confidence that I could do it.

Finally came the financial settlement, and I had more money than I'd ever dreamed of. I remember the exact amount of the check—$465,021.75. Don't ask me about the $21 or the $0.75. I have no idea how they arrived at that amount, and I didn't care. That was a fortune back then.

All of a sudden, law school was realistic, and I started planning for it. But all my forward planning made my bachelor's degree work harder, and my grades fell off. I'd gotten all As and Bs up till then but ended up with a couple of Cs in my last year.

Mr. Farlow had gone to Rutgers Law School over in Newark; he helped me get admitted there. I took a year's leave of absence from the law firm at his suggestion and enrolled. It's a good thing I didn't know what I was in for. If I had, I wouldn't have done it. It was hard, especially the first year.

When I look back on those years, I'm amazed at myself. Getting through college was difficult, but law school was much harder. I wanted to quit almost every day during the first semester, but it wasn't only the academic challenges; there was no one else like me in my class. There were two other women, but they were twenty-two years old, single, and right out of college. One was an African American woman from Newark who had grown up and gone to school in New York City. I felt completely alone. At home, I was always studying. Rachel and Sammy didn't have a mother that year, and Sam didn't have a wife. God bless them. They weren't happy with me, but they hung in there. Mr. Farlow was great too. He'd check in with me every couple of weeks and encourage me to keep going.

It took about six months for things to begin to click. In about March of that first academic year, I began to get a feel for the material, learned to think in legal terms. Before March, I had to stretch my brain to reach a glimmer of understanding. It felt as though I was reading through gauze. But that spring, the fuzziness dissipated.

It took four years, but I completed the program, and on my second try, I passed the Pennsylvania Bar exam. I had gone back to the law firm part time after the second year and returned full time after finishing.

During my first few years as a practicing lawyer, I focused mostly on family law—divorces, child custody, and estates. Occasionally, I'd get an automobile-accident liability case to handle. That was the way it worked at the firm; you "paid your dues" for a while after you joined the practice and worked to develop your own cases. Partly because of my involvement with the Minisink Environmental Defense group started by Loretta Shuster, I developed an interest in environment law. There wasn't much legal work in that area back in the 1970s, and Mr. Farlow and the other partners were skeptical that environmental law was a viable specialty for us.

My big break came when I acquired a case against the owners of a coal mine over by Girardville. The mine had been inactive for some years, but the owners hadn't done due diligence when they stopped operations. The site was dangerous and unsightly, and the owners of nearby homes claimed the foundations of their houses were cracking because of previous mine operations and the failure to shut it down properly. Then a ten-year-old boy was killed in a fall while he and some friends were playing at the site; two other boys were hurt. I organized a half-dozen families in the area and filed suit against the coal company. This case was a lucrative one for the firm and the families. After that, the firm went all out to help me build an environmental law program.

Things were going well in my legal career but not at home. Sam and I weren't communicating. I began to think I'd "outgrown" him. But I admit I wasn't investing much of myself at home. For a few years, it was only Sam, Rachel, and Sammy at the dinner table most nights. On many nights, I came home from work after the dinner dishes were done, had a couple of drinks, took a shower, got my clothes ready for the next day, and went to bed. I was asleep before Sam came to bed and gone in the morning before he came down for breakfast. We hardly talked.

Most bothersome was my affair with one of the young lawyers at the firm. Josh was handsome, a still-fit college lacrosse player, and oversexed. It only lasted a few months, but it was torrid. Sometimes we'd rent a motel room for a few hours during the day and spend it screwing. A couple of times a month, I'd tell Sam I had to stay overnight in Scranton to prepare for a trial, and we'd spend the night together. I knew Josh and I wouldn't be together long term; we shared sex, not love. I don't think the word "love" ever passed between us. I believe too that he was seeing other women while he and I were involved.

Mr. Farlow rescued me—again. He called me into his office one day after I had come back from a couple of hours with Josh. Uncharacteristically, Mr. Farlow was uncomfortable, and when I looked him full in the face, his discomfort was evident. I was alarmed, thought something bad had happened, that his wife or one of his children had an accident. He started to speak but couldn't get the words out. I wanted to go around his desk to comfort him but sat and waited.

He took a deep breath. "Holly…Holly, I believe we are all entitled to personal privacy."

I was confused, still hadn't made the connection between Josh, me, and my presence in Mr. Farlow's office. "Yes…" I said.

"But there comes a time," he continued, sounding more businesslike. "Josh Barnett is not a moral man. It's clear what is happening between you two. Everyone here knows; it's become the main gossip in the office. I must say, Holly, I'm disappointed. It's not worthy of you."

I was stunned and then mortified. Then the thought came: *My God, if everyone here knows, does Sam know too?*

Mr. Farlow continued, in control; he asked gently, "Do you want to say anything?"

Now I was the uncomfortable one, unable to speak. Mr. Farlow waited. I looked at him. His face was sympathetic. "I'm sorry" was all I could say.

We sat quietly for a moment.

"I'm ashamed," I said.

"I know, Holly. You're better than this."

Then I had a real cry. Mr. Farlow slid a box of tissues across to me and waited.

When I regained control, I said, "I don't know what else to say."

"I think more conversation can wait. I have a couple of things to say, though. First, your job is not in jeopardy now. I'm going to talk to Josh and suggest he will be better off elsewhere—perhaps at one of the large law firms in Philadelphia. I'll help him find a spot and give him a good recommendation. I think he can be a good lawyer, but this is not the place for him. I'll give him a small severance. Second, when we finish our conversation today, I want you to leave, take Thursday and Friday off. When you come in Monday, you and I will talk at ten a.m. Try to relax and clear your head. I think this whole thing can be a blip on the radar. I'm going to leave my office for a few minutes. When I'm gone, get yourself together, go to your office, get your things, and leave. Okay?"

I nodded my agreement.

It was a long ride home. When I got there, the house was empty, and I was mentally exhausted and physically sick. I undressed and went to bed. I heard Sammy come in from school but could not find the energy to get up. Then, Sam came to our bedroom in the late afternoon. He came and stood beside me. I was afraid to open my eyes.

In a low voice, he asked, "Are you okay?"

"Yes. I'm not feeling well."

"Shall I call the doctor?" His voice was worried.

"No, I think I got some bad seafood at lunch. But I'm starting to feel better."

"Can I bring you something? Hot tea? Some soup?"

"Thank you; no. I'll come down at dinner, but I'll just have some tea."

"I'll get it ready and let you know."

I felt shame, and my tears flowed again. It was hard to go down to dinner when Sam called, but I forced myself. It was Sam, Sam Jr., and me at the table; Rachel had married. We were quiet, and it felt awkward. Our conversation was stilted.

When Sam and Sammy finished eating, they got up from the table and began cleaning up. I stood to help but realized I didn't know the routine. Sam was filling the sink with warm soapy water, and Sammy was scraping plates and stacking the dirty dishes beside the sink. I put the butter and milk into the refrigerator but could not see a next step, so I went upstairs to the bedroom. I hoped Sam would come, but he did not. I could hear occasional conversation and laughter from the two of them when they reacted to the television. Sam came to bed about 9:30 p.m. I feigned sleep and lay there until I was sure he was asleep. Then I went down to the dark empty living room and sat on the couch. Soon I was sleepy, found the comforter we kept in the living room, and laid down. I awoke to the sound of Sam's alarm clock at 6:30 a.m. I went to the kitchen and made coffee.

Sam came downstairs first. "How do you feel this morning?"

"Better but not good. I won't go to work."

"Good. I hope you can rest. Is there anything I can do? Anything you need?"

"I think I'll be fine. I'm going to eat a little."

Sammy came down, book bag in hand. He was ready to leave for the school bus. "Morning, Dad. How are you feelin', Mom?"

He didn't sound like a child. "I'm much better, Sammy. Thank you." I watched them go through their routine and felt estranged. He quickly prepared and ate a bowl of cold breakfast cereal.

Sam left first after kissing me on the cheek. Sammy left a few minutes later with a simple "Bye, Mom." I sat at the kitchen table for a long time, feeling, *I'm not part of my son's life.*

It was a quiet few days for me. I mostly read and napped. Sam took Sammy to a friend's house late Saturday morning. In the afternoon, he cut the lawn and cleaned the gutters. I watched him work, heard him on the roof. He seemed contented. Late on Saturday, he went to pick Sammy up from his friend's house. I listened to their chatter as they came into the house. When Sam started to prepare dinner, he asked, "Is your stomach ready for real food?"

"My stomach's fine, and I'm starved."

"Great. I am too. In fact, I'll cut some cheese for us to nibble while I cook."

I sat at the kitchen table with a book but mostly watched him cook pork chops in a large skillet. He boiled potatoes, cut them up, and added them to the skillet with seasoning. The he got a bag of peas and carrots from the freezer and prepared the entire bag.

I got up and set the table. The normality of it all hit me hard, and I had to retreat upstairs for another cry. Later that night when we went to bed, I was struck by the absence of physical intimacy, and for a few minutes, I worried that I'd have to leave the bed to cry again.

I woke up Sunday feeling better and prepared a large breakfast but still felt a stranger while we ate.

When we had finished eating, Sam said, "They're having a flea market with some music up at Dingmans's Ferry today. Would you like to go check it out?"

"That sounds great," I said.

"Can I go too?" Sammy asked.

"I was hoping you would," answered Sam.

"I'll bet they'll have one of those cotton-candy machines."

"I'll bet they do too," I said.

It was a delightful afternoon, and we snacked and did not want dinner when we got home. Watching my husband and son and the simple, sometimes silly, goings-on at the market, I had decided. I stopped Sam in the vestibule as we came into the house, put my arms around him, and whispered in his ear, "That was wonderful,

Sam. I want to say too that I am going to change some things—work less, spend more time at home. Will you help me?"

He grabbed me so hard that it took my breath away. He didn't speak, but I didn't need to hear words.

When I met with Mr. Farlow Monday morning, I was still ashamed.

"Are you ready to get back to work?"

"I am. I apologize, Mr. Farlow. My behavior was unacceptable."

"Okay. We don't have to discuss that again. But while you and Josh were cavorting, you were distracted, and it was evident in the quality of your work. You have not brought a new case to the firm in almost a year. That has to change."

I was a bit taken aback by his bluntness but later felt that it struck just the right tone and was grateful for the clarity.

Mr. Farlow disregarded my discomfort and went on. "Let's discuss your current caseload and where else I expect you to focus in the next six months."

He knew every case I was handling and asked about the details of each one. Occasionally, he made a suggestion. He advised that I back off on one of my more active cases against a coal company on behalf of a construction contractor who found a building site they hoped to build on contaminated so badly that the county would not issue a building permit.

"Don't call them. If they call you, don't call them back right away; wait a few days. They're going to want to settle this fiscal year. Wait a few months and then tell them we've decided to file suit. Refuse to discuss details and then wait. I think they'll respond with a decent offer, but we'll use that as a starting point."

I spent almost two hours in Mr. Farlow's office that Monday morning, growing more comfortable as my focus shifted from my behavior with Josh to the details of my legal work. After the meeting, I passed Josh's office on the way to my own office. It was dark, and his nameplate had been removed from the door.

It stayed uncomfortable at work for a while. My interactions with some people were strained. Mr. Farlow's secretary, an older, blue-haired, churchgoing matron, was especially judgmental and made sure I noticed. But in less than a month, things got back to normal, except for one young legal technician who would occasionally try to engage me in a discussion about my affair with Josh. I finally asked her if she would like Josh's telephone number, and that shut her up.

It took a while at home too as I struggled to find a new balance with work. I had to accept finally that I simply could not be home by 6:00 p.m. every day and sometimes had to be away overnight. The job-home tension never fully resolved, but it helped that I was earning a very good income, and I really liked being an accomplished professional.

For a while, I struggled with guilt about my affair and uncertainty about how and whether to deal with the empty state of our marriage. I'd decided I would not bring up my affair with Josh with Sam but that I would be honest with him if he asked or seemed interested in an explicit discussion about the reasons for what I believed had been a protracted estrangement between us. I was ready to accept primary responsibility for the estrangement. I ruminated for days about what I should do or whether I should simply let things unfold. I was convinced that if there was to be a discussion, I'd have to initiate it; I knew Sam would not.

Finally, I decided the empty phase of our marriage needed to be addressed. If not, I thought, it would always hang in the air between us. I waited for an opportunity to start a conversation with Sam, but none appeared naturally. I got impatient, so one Friday night after dinner, when Sammy was out with his friends, sitting in the living room watching some silly sitcom, I said, "Sam, I'd like to have a talk about us."

He continued looking at the television screen. He took a deep breath.

I waited, and when he didn't speak, I asked, "Sam, will you look at me?"

He turned to face to me, but his eyes did not engage. I waited.

"I don't know what to say, Holly."

"Will you talk with me?" I asked softly.

"Yes, I want to talk to you."

"I don't know where to begin either, Sam."

He nodded. I continued, "We haven't been separated formally, but we've been apart together. I don't want that to continue."

Sam seemed as if he was going to say something but simply sighed.

I continued, "I know I've been inconsiderate, absent a lot because of my work."

"You can say that again." His voice was hard.

His anger stunned me, and I didn't say anything right away. "I don't begrudge your anger, Sam, but do you want to try to fix things?"

"I didn't break anything."

After another silence, I said, "We don't have to talk right now, Sam, but just tell me, shall we try to make things better between us? I want to. But it's not a one-person job. We need to do it together."

We sat quietly for several minutes. Then, I said, "I'm going to get ready for bed, Sam. Like I said, we don't have to have a long, heavy conversation right now, but sometime soon I'd like you to tell me whether you want to talk about things. I don't think we can pretend everything's okay between us."

I got up to leave when Sam said, "I want things to be better with us." His voice was less angry. "But I'm tired right now, not up for it."

"That's okay. I can wait."

He nodded—really did look tired or dejected.

"I do love you, Sam."

He looked at me and tried to smile but couldn't quite make it happen.

Sam and I had two long talks. Both were difficult. Sam was angry, and I finally realized, still sorting things out in his head. During the first talk, he wasn't hearing what I said. Reflecting on that conversation afterward, I realized we were talking past each other. I was relieved that my sexual infidelity didn't seem to be an issue but later realized it was lurking off to the side.

Things improved slowly. We started talking, first awkwardly and then more naturally. I knew we had turned a corner when we laughed together one evening in the kitchen. We both recognized the moment and hugged. It was then that I felt we would be all right. But there was a subsequent conversation that set us back.

That conversation was contentious. On the surface, it seemed to be about things that shouldn't be that hard to resolve: Sammy's curfew time on weekends, hiring a housekeeper to clean once every week or two, and some other stuff I don't even remember.

We were in the living room again, sitting across from each other, when, out of the blue, Sam said, "I got laid a couple of times."

I was stunned speechless, unusual for me. Finally, I said, "What the hell does that mean?"

"Just what I said."

"You son of a bitch. You're not going to drop a bomb like that and think I'm going to just let it go."

"Well, I'm not going to say any more about it."

It seemed so out of character for Sam that I said, "Is this a joke?"

"It's no joke."

"Well, you bastard. You're not sleepin' in my bed tonight."

"Fine with me," he said.

I lay awake almost all night—finally fell asleep after 4:00 a.m. and woke up late. The house was quiet. Sammy's book bag was gone, and so was Sam's truck. I was sure he hadn't taken a shower or changed his clothes. He must have worn the same clothes to work he wore the day before.

He came home late after work. I was in the kitchen making an omelet for Sammy and me. He came to the kitchen door and asked, "Can I talk to you?"

Sammy was up in his room, but I was afraid how our conversation might go, so I turned off the burner and said, "Let's go to the garage."

He followed me there. I stood, my arms folded across my chest.

"I'm sorry," he said. "I acted like an asshole last night."

He half sat on a tall stool in front of his workbench.

"That's not good enough," I said and waited. He looked horrible. His face drooped, and his hair and clothes were disheveled. He looked at me—helpless.

I softened a little. "Sam, you can't simply announce sexual infidelity and expect to leave it at that. What do you expect from me? I should pat you on the head like a naughty boy and tell you not to do that again?"

"I'm sorry, Holly. I didn't get laid." He looked miserable.

I was flummoxed. "This can't be the end of it, Sam. You better get yourself together and tell me the truth. And don't wait too long."

A couple of days later, he came to me to say he was ready to talk but asked if we could go to his cabin to do so. He looked much better, unhappy, but I could see the real Sam underneath.

We sat in his "living room," which was a laugh. The room was furnished with a mishmash of chairs of different styles and colors. There was no couch or coffee table and only one homemade end table.

"I really didn't get laid—I came close to starting something with somebody but backed away. It wasn't out of any love or loyalty to you. I knew it would complicate things and decided I wasn't up for it. I hated it when we had to sneak around."

I said, "This is an ugly room, Sam."

He looked around. "Yeah, it is, isn't it?"

In the silence, a dark realization began to overtake me. I felt the color drain from my face. I wanted to lie down and resisted an urge to lie on the floor. At that moment, I realized. *He knows. Oh my God! He knows.* It felt like someone pushing down on my shoulders, forcing me lower in my seat. I forced myself to look at him. His rocking chair moved gently back and forth. But his stare was unrelenting. I never saw that look from him before, and never since.

"You know, Sam, don't you? You know."

He nodded but didn't speak.

"I did get laid." I couldn't hold my head up; I leaned forward, my elbows on my thighs. Sam was quiet. I forced myself to look into his face. His demeanor was steely.

"How long have you known?"

He was thoughtful, calm. "I'm not sure, exactly. Not for too long."

We were quiet several minutes.

"Is there anything you want to know? Anything you'd like me to do?"

He didn't respond right away. "No, I don't think so. You may have said all you need to. But I'll think about it."

I wanted badly to put my arms around him, especially feel his arms around me. But I knew that could not—should not—happen then.

We were somber for a time, quiet. I think, for about a week. Sammy sensed our mood, and true to his paternal roots, he was quiet too.

Sam came to our bedroom one night. I was sitting up, reading. He closed the bedroom door and sat in the chair across from me. I closed my book.

"I have two questions. First, are you still seeing someone? And, can you assure me it will not happen again?"

"I'd like to say a couple of things before I answer, Sam."

"Okay."

"I am very sorry, profoundly sorry. The last thing I wanted to do was hurt you, and I know I've done that."

"Thank you."

"I am not involved with anyone now and never will be again."

He nodded, his shoulders relaxed. "I have forgiven you, Holly. I believe too that your promise of fidelity is sincere. I'm still hurting. I think it's trust. I'm wary."

I was struck by the clarity in his statement; it seemed unlike him. But it was reassuring too. It told me he was certain about his feelings.

"I can understand that," I said. I was afraid to ask the question on my mind but steeled myself and said, "Do you think you can trust me again?"

He was thoughtful. "Yes, I think so…I do. I love you."

"I love you, Sam. I want to be with you forever."

"I think it'll just take a little time."

It did take time for Sam and me to find our way back to a comfortable intimacy. Sam and I never talked about sex. For us it had always been an intimate conversation wrapped in intense physical pleasure but without words. We were both awkward in bed during the reconnection time. I recognized too that sex between Sam and I would not be like it was in the beginning, nor would it match the feverish intensity of my trysts with Josh. In the process, Sam became a patient lover, and I did too. Eventually we were satisfied and happy in bed. I felt Sam really did trust me. We never spoke of my affair again, and I had no sense it lingered with Sam either.

Will Mead

The last year or two at Cloud Farm was a difficult period for me personally. I felt an obligation to the community to keep going, and I loved living in the Minisink Valley. The scenic magnificence of the place lifted my spirit. But the constant economic pressure, the animosity of the local community, and the expectation that I be the arbiter of personal disputes among community members eroded my spirit. Something subtler began to weigh on me too: I missed the intellectual stimulation of academic life. I was happy and felt nourished in college, graduate school, and during my short stint on the faculty at NYU. I had underestimated how much I would miss academia.

The university campus is populated by individuals who generate new ideas and attempt to be at the cutting edge of their fields of study. My primary interest was sociology, but over the years, I discovered the boundaries of this and other disciplines are permeable. Anthropologists study many of the same things that sociologists do—how and why social groups are formed, their purposes, and the function of their rules and rituals. Most anthropologists at that time studied early societies, and my focus was on contemporary ones, but there were parallels, and each perspective has insights to offer the other. I had a geologist friend back at NYU and was delighted when I discovered that he was studying the relationship between the physical characteristics of the land and the organization of society. Physical setting affects social organization.

I had brought books with me to Cloud Farm but found it difficult to keep up with new developments in sociology. Publishing companies no longer sent me free copies of their latest textbooks in the hope that I would adopt them for my classes. There was rarely extra money to buy new books. I used the library in Stroudsburg, but the collection didn't match my interests very well. Also, I was so busy with Cloud Farm activities that I couldn't spend much time reading or at the library.

From the outset, Cloud Farm and those who lived there were viewed with hostility by local folks. All along, we tried to minimize our interactions with the locals. This helped to maintain the peace. But about a year and a half before our experiment ended for good, a situation developed that was dangerous.

One afternoon, a short convoy of four vehicles pulled into my driveway. Rosemary saw them coming from the kitchen window and called to me. I went to meet them. The lead vehicle was an old pickup with two men in the cab. The second, also a pickup truck with three male passengers in the cab and several in the back. The third was a station wagon with a half-dozen men and the fourth a full-size sedan, also occupied by four or five men. Altogether fifteen to eighteen men, uninvited, in our driveway.

Nervously, I walked toward the first pickup. A middle-age man, tall and wiry, got out of the truck. He wore denim overalls, and my eyes were drawn to his hands, which seemed large for the rest of his physique. No one else exited the vehicles.

"Are you Will Mead?" His tone was hostile; he didn't offer to shake hands.

"I am."

"You're the boss?"

"No, not the boss. But I do try to keep things organized around here."

He looked around. "We're looking for Kyle Manness."

I didn't recognize the name. "He stays here?" I asked. I racked my brain to connect a face or another name with Kyle Manness.

"You're damned right he stays here. Scrawny little son of a bitch, long hair, long beard. Always wears sandals."

It came to me. "Oh, Kyle. I couldn't remember his last name. He doesn't stay here at this house. I think he's staying with the McKoys for now."

"Where are the McKoys?"

The McKoys' house was only a quarter-mile away, but I didn't want to send these angry-looking men there without attempting to problem solve or defuse whatever was on their minds.

"I think they're away for a few days, but maybe I can help."

"We want Kyle Manness."

"I don't think he's around either, but I'll see if I can locate him for you."

"If you're the boss, why don't you know where your people are?"

"I'm not the kind of boss you think." He was suspicious that I was hiding Kyle Manness.

"Well, I guess we'll just go find him ourselves." He turned to go.

"I think I can help you, sir. If you can tell me a little more."

He stared at me. "Your Kyle is a thief. He might be dangerous too."

I barely knew Kyle, and my image of him was of a mild, quiet young man.

"How about I do this, Mr....I'm sorry. I don't know your name."

"Weber. Jim Weber."

"We don't want thieves in our community and certainly don't want to harbor anyone who is dangerous."

"We want to see Kyle face-to-face."

"Okay. I'll make that happen. But I really don't know where he is right now. Can you give me some time to locate him?"

"Wait a minute." He walked back to his truck and spoke to his passenger. Then he and the passenger walked back to the station wagon.

I watched as the men gathered in a cluster and conferred. After a few minutes, Jim Weber came back to me.

"We'll come back here tomorrow at the same time and expect to see Kyle Manness. Can you have him here?"

I knew I wasn't going to comply, but I answered, "I'll have Kyle Manness here tomorrow, same time."

I gathered several of our group and Kyle Manness, and we met in my living room that night. Kyle tried to evade our questions but finally acknowledged a few things. He was hanging out at the local high school and selling marijuana to some of those kids. He had also been caught shoplifting at a local market and had stolen some books at the library. He also acknowledged there was a budding romance between him and a local girl but swore it hadn't progressed to the sex yet.

We satisfied ourselves that Kyle was a minor offender and not dangerous. But he was surely a danger to the rest of us. We understood too that many of the local people were looking for a chance to do away entirely with our community. Kyle Manness could be an excuse for major aggression against all of us. We decided to banish Kyle.

The next morning, I borrowed Sam Kopco's pickup truck, drove Kyle to Allentown, bought him a ticket on the first bus to New York City, and watched him leave before I returned to Cloud Farm.

That afternoon when Jim Weber and a smaller group of men came to my house expecting to find Kyle Manness, we had a delicate situation. Three of us met Jim Weber and two other men. We had concocted a story—that the previous day, before we were aware that Kyle had been involved in the activities Jim Weber had brought to our attention, Kyle had asked Dan McKoy to take him to the bus terminal, where someone had arranged for a ticket to New York City. Kyle had taken that bus, and we had verified that he was in New York as of last night. Kyle must have guessed he was in trouble and left town.

They did not believe our story, of course. One of the men with Jim Weber was especially threatening. As we stood behind my house talking, he removed a long ax handle from his pant leg and made sure we noticed the weapon. He waved it around when he talked. We finally satisfied the group of men when we allowed them to search my house and Dan McKoy's house and assured them that we would let them know if Kyle Manness returned. Some of the men were still grumbling when they left, but that was the end of the episode as far as I could tell. We never saw or heard from Kyle again.

Over time, the physical challenges, economic pressure, administrative duties, and intellectual isolation ate away at my commitment to Cloud Farm.

Then, I had a personal visit at the farm from an Army Corps of Engineers official. He didn't seem overtly threatening, but I thought it was ominous. To my knowledge he was the only federal-government official with authority who ever saw Cloud Farm in person. I felt sure too that our failure to pay rent and electric bills would eventually bring a concerted effort to evict us. As my commitment to the project eroded, the group's commitment faded too. One of our original families went back to New York.

Bob and Elizabeth Fields were close friends with Rosemary and me. They were both employed by New York City: Bob in social services and Elizabeth as a librarian. Bob had vacationed with his family in the Delaware Water Gap area as a boy. He had great memories of those years, especially swimming in the Delaware River and canoeing on it. Elizabeth grew up in a small town in southern Ohio and had become involved in the peace movement in college. She was a wonderful quilter; her quilts sold for $200 or more in the arts-and-crafts store in East Stroudsburg that catered to tourists. They moved from New York to Cloud Farm with us on day one and had worked just as hard as we did to get the enterprise going.

Bob and Liz both believed in what we were attempting to do—build a self-sustaining utopian community. They were quiet people. If something needed to be done, you could count on Bob to take care of it. One time, we decided we should have an outside shed so that we could store tools—mostly hand implements, but we had managed to get a motorized lawn mower and garden tiller too. About a week after we talked about a shed, Bob came by to get me to show me the shed, built in a clearing in the woods on the far side of his house. I'd heard hammering off and on for a couple of days prior but hadn't paid much attention. I was stunned.

"How did you do this? Where did you get the wood?"

Bob was smiling. "There was some unused lumber under our house. And you know that site north on three oh nine where they're building several houses—about three to four miles out?"

"I think so."

"I borrowed some of their lumber. The boards don't fit together too well, but our stuff will be sheltered from the worst of the weather."

It was true. The boards on the shed didn't match, and there were gaps between them, but Bob had put together a woodshed with a flat roof about six feet by eight feet.

"The door doesn't fit very well, and it's hard to open and close, but I think I can improve that."

I looked at the door hinges and latch. "Where did you get the hardware? Did you steal that too?"

"No, I bought the nails and hinges at the hardware store in town. Cost less than ten dollars."

I was delighted. "This calls for a celebration," I said.

We sat on my back porch and smoked a joint.

I was devastated when they left. In character, they left quietly during the night. I noticed there was no activity at their house the next morning but didn't think much about it.

That afternoon Rosemary came to me. "I think Bob and Liz are gone."

We went to their house. It was empty, except for some large furniture items in the living room and their queen-size bed upstairs. Closets and cabinets were empty. There was only a half quart of milk in the refrigerator. I looked for a note; there was none. We felt bereft. I held Rosemary while she sobbed.

Later, Rosemary told me that Liz was pregnant and concerned that she would not get prenatal care or proper attention when the baby was born. She'd had a miscarriage during an earlier pregnancy. It was several years before we saw them again. They were apologetic about the manner of their departure from Cloud Farm and obviously uncomfortable. They were living in Brooklyn with their healthy little girl and firmly reestablished with social welfare and librarian jobs.

Rosemary and I had gotten over our feelings of betrayal and were interested to rekindle our friendship. We got together a few more times but could never get close again. They were in touch when Rosemary died, but our former intimacy was absent.

Sam Kopco came by to visit occasionally when he was working in the area. I really enjoyed his company. We'd sit on the porch above the river, smoke a joint, and talk. Sam isn't an intellectual, but he's enjoyable to be with. He didn't talk much about his Vietnam experience, but I could tell it weighed on him. Sam is the only local friend I made during the years we lived in the Minisink Valley.

One night, when I knew the end was near for Cloud Farm, sitting in the dark on my porch over the river, I told Sam, "I have appreciated your help, Sam, especially that night when you turned the electric on so we could get a doctor out here."

"Glad I could help."

"You could've lost your job."

"I doubt it. My boss wouldn't fire me for that."

"It was important. Two lives may have been lost."

Sam didn't respond right away. I thought the conversation was over when he spoke again. "One thing I learned in the army: you got to be there when the chips are down."

It dawned on me that night that Sam was a quiet version of my father. He was a blue-collar guy too—a steelworker—but not like Sam. My father scared me when I was young; had a short temper; he shouted a lot. We had a nice, friendly relationship after I finished college, but, unfortunately, I never really got to know him before he died. A heart attack got him right before he was set to retire. I was grateful to have gotten to know Sam.

Our attempt to build a back-to-the-earth, self-sustaining community in northeastern Pennsylvania ended abruptly on a bitterly cold February morning in 1974. While it was still dark, a combined federal/state/local police task force evicted us forcibly from our homes along the Delaware River. Young children and a newborn were among the displaced; no arrangements for shelter from the harsh elements were made. We were unable to care for our farm animals, and most of them disappeared or died from starvation. We tried to engage the courts on our behalf, but the authorities had anticipated this attempt, and government attorneys were ready with their counterarguments. Decades later, the bitterness I felt for months afterward still rankles just below the surface.

It's clear to me now that a final eviction was inevitable. A few things kept a spark of hope alive, but looking back, I was naïve about our situation. There had been previous eviction attempts that we managed to resist, and we had begun to find support among a few environmentalists in the area. One of our attorneys from Philadelphia had driven up to warn us just after midnight on the day we were evicted. I believed that the final eviction action would be like the previous ones—only partially effective—and that we could weather the temporary storm. But this time the eviction planning had been meticulous.

While we slept, a collection of federal, state, and local law enforcement surrounded our compound to keep the press and other witnesses away. We had foiled an earlier attempt by climbing onto the roofs of our houses, and the authorities called off the bulldozers that were poised to raze the buildings. This time the task force made sure we could not react. They came in the dark with overwhelming force.

It was frightening. I had been awake when they arrived but did not expect what was about to happen until I heard the first boots on my porch. I was blinded by floodlights when I opened the door. I was in handcuffs, hands behind my back, face down on the frozen ground before I understood how determined the authorities were. I couldn't identify who was attacking us and worried that it might be a vigilante group of residents. I remember the boots and the shouting. Occasionally I would catch a glimpse of an unfamiliar face or the flash of a badge, but most had scarves drawn across their faces. I spotted a US Marshal's service uniform at one point. They didn't look like the riot police I see on TV nowadays, with their helmets, plastic face guards, and rubber bullets, but we were still terrified.

The image that sticks in my mind is that of my wife and daughter standing on our porch shivering in their nightgowns. Standing behind them in the doorway to keep them out of the house stood a large figure, hands folded across his chest. Only his eyes were visible above the scarf across his face.

They took us to a large storage facility, where they kept county-road repair equipment. It was cold inside, but at least there was no wind. Initially there were only a few of us. I did not know what had happened to Rosemary and Diana. Within about two hours, though, we were all there. Rosemary had managed to get Diana's winter coat on her, but neither she nor I were dressed for the weather. Few of us had coats or hats, and none of us had gloves. We sat on the cold concrete shivering for a couple of hours before someone arrived with a load of blankets. There were not enough blankets for everyone, so we had to share.

We were sheltered from the wind but in real physical danger from the cold before several church vans began arriving to take us to the social hall in the basement of the Lutheran church in town. Our first day and night there were difficult. We were warm, but it took a day for the church and other charitable people in the area to gather blankets, pillows, and cots to sleep on and to set up a kitchen to feed us.

The lawyer who had driven up from Philadelphia to warn us tried to get the court to intervene, but his hastily drawn-up petition for a temporary stay of the eviction was denied.

Gradually, we found places to go. Most could identify relatives or friends to house us temporarily. Some of us stayed there a week. Eventually, Rosemary, Diana, and I went to my mother's home on Staten Island. Sam Kopco drove us there.

The next half year was a stressful time. We were crowded at my mom's house, and Rosemary and my mother did not get along. Mom would not let Rosemary help with the cooking, and her housecleaning was not up to my mother's standards. Fortunately, sociology was a very popular college major in those years, so I was rehired to an assistant professor's position at NYU. We moved into our own apartment in September, and I resumed teaching. Rosemary found a job at a music store, and we enrolled Diana in the second grade. It took Diana several months to adjust to the regimentation in school, but she finally settled down. By the time she reached eighth grade, she was an academic star.

After two years back in urban life and the academic environment, memories of the Cloud Farm years faded. I did find an academic use for the experience, though. In a graduate course, I taught on Forms of Human Organization and incorporated my experience at Cloud Farm into the course material—mainly in discussion of impediments to organizational success.

I wrote a book about the Cloud Farm years but could not find a publisher. I still have the manuscript. I've been thinking about writing a memoir of my life but have not developed a coherent plan for it. If I ever do a memoir, the story of my Cloud Farm years would find a place in that book; it might even be the entire book…

Epilogue: May 2018

Strike another match, go start anew
And it's all over now, Baby Blue

> Bob Dylan
> *It's All Over Now, Baby Blue* (1965)

Sam

It wasn't worth the damage done to the people who lost their homes, but the Minisink Valley came out of the Tocks Island Dam years in good shape. After a long period of turmoil and uncertainty, the National Park Service turned the area that would have been taken up by the dam and adjacent land into the Delaware Water Gap National Recreation Area, a seventy-thousand-acre natural area that includes a forty-mile section of the middle Delaware River, one hundred miles of hiking trails, and the most beautiful natural mountain and forest area I've ever seen.

I don't hike much anymore. I'm still in good shape, but the scar tissue and shrapnel from Vietnam makes my left leg drag when I get tired and caused me to fall a couple of times. I just got scraped up in the falls, but I decided not to push my luck. I like to hike alone, so if I fell out there and broke a bone or cracked my skull, I might lay there a long time before anybody found me.

I'm happier than I've ever been. I wish Holly wasn't so busy, though. I hoped we would travel together when I retired, maybe even get an RV, and drive across the country for six months or a year. She shot that idea down right away—wouldn't even consider the idea of taking short trips in an RV. I got her to take a ten-day Caribbean cruise a couple of years ago, and it was great for three or four days. After that she was on the phone half the time talking to her office staff or somebody in Philadelphia or Washington. I got so pissed that I couldn't wait to get back home.

We've figured out how to get away together and enjoy it. The destination is key. I would be happy on the Appalachian Trail for a week, but Holly prefers to travel to a city or someplace that has interesting historical and cultural attractions. We both like good food and music, so that's nice. I like some museums. I'm not crazy about art museums like she is, but I like some. The Spy Museum in Washington and the World War II Museum in New Orleans, battlefields; guess I'm drawn back to 'Nam no matter where I go. We keep the trips to less than a week, though. Holly can tolerate four or five days away from her practice but not many more. Truth is, I don't like being away from home for very long either.

Rachel has brought more joy to me than anyone. She took to me as a little girl, and after Holly and I married, she decided, without any prompting from me or Holly, that she should start calling me Daddy. I was delighted, but Holly wasn't so sure. For a while clever Rachel called me Daddy when she and I were alone together and Mr. Kopco when her mother was there. That didn't go on for long, though. One day, just a month or two into the marriage, at the dinner table one night, Holly announced that Rachel could call me Daddy, but she should not pretend that I was her real father.

I had to stifle a smile when Rachel said, "I know that, Mother. You and Mr. Kopco didn't make me. You and Mark did. So I'll call Mark Father and Mr. Kopco Daddy."

Holly put her fork down, stared at Rachel, started to say something, changed her mind, and went back to her meal. That was the end of it. I still smile when I think of that moment.

I used to think that Holly was the most together person I've ever known, but over the years, watching Rachel navigate life, I've decided she is. Her instincts are spot-on, and there is a natural kindness about her. The kindness instinct was a problem at times when she was growing up. She wanted to care for every injured or homeless pet within fifty miles, so we had to impose limits that made her unhappy. She pushed back for a long time, but by about fourteen, she understood the need for these limits.

Her instinct to help anyone in her orbit who was having trouble brought us frequent dinner and holiday guests, sometimes creating awkward situations. One sad situation involved a classmate whose father was beating her mother. Rachel brought this girl home and tried to get us to make a report to the police. We managed to get the county social-welfare people involved without getting caught in the middle. For a long time, Rachel didn't see why it was usually not smart to intervene into other's family difficulties. It's no surprise that, for a while, Rachel ran a local nonprofit that provided emergency assistance to families in need.

I had some rocky times with my son, Sam Jr. Sammy was a good kid but different from what I expected. It took a long time for me to understand and accept that. And who finally set me straight? You guessed it—Rachel.

My hope was that Sammy was going to be a great athlete. I thought I was being wise and insightful by deciding early that I would not try to make him a wrestler because people would always be comparing him to me, and that could be hard for him. Sammy's body type, I decided early, was best suited to be a baseball shortstop or basketball guard. So, by the time he was eight or nine, I sent him to baseball and basketball camps and signed him up to play these youth sports.

Sammy was never a complainer and usually went along with whatever plans you made for him, but he was not very competitive, and his natural hand-eye coordination, an attribute that was key to the sports and positions I had picked for him, was average for a long time. By the time he was twelve or thirteen, it was obvious that he was not on track to be a star athlete. I decided he was not practicing enough and needed to push himself harder and began to pressure him to do more. I even hired a sports psychologist from East Stroudsburg University's phys-ed department to work with him.

Looking back, I can see this is when the tension between me and Sammy started. He didn't want to be a star athlete, didn't want to spend all his free time trying to improve his athletic skills. Then, in sophomore year of high school, he refused to sign up for baseball, and I showed my ass.

After work one day, I went to watch the baseball team practice. Sammy wasn't there, so I talked to the coach, who told me he had decided not to play. I went home and found him, his girlfriend, and another young couple sitting on our front porch drinking beer. They all scrambled into the house as I came down the driveway. I found them in the kitchen trying to hide the empty beer cans. I was furious. Not about the fifteen-year-old kids drinking beer, I'm embarrassed today to say that my first reaction was to shout at Sammy.

"Why aren't you at baseball practice?"

Silence.

While his friends scrambled out of the house, Sammy turned and walked back to his bedroom.

I followed, furious. I hardly remember what I said to him, but it was ugly. I think I called him a quitter; I hope that's the worst thing I said. He sat on the edge of his bed, silent. Then he laid back, hands behind his head, staring at the ceiling, still not responding to my shouted questions. I came close to hitting him.

I shouted, "Why aren't you at baseball practice?"

More silence.

"Answer me," I said, even louder.

"I have nothing to say except I'm not playing baseball."

"Why?"

"Because I don't want to."

"That's not good enough," I said.

"It's good enough for me." With that, he rolled over, turned his back to me.

I was shaking with anger but thankfully saw the futility of my words, left his bedroom, and took a long walk in the woods behind our house.

Our relationship went into a deep freeze after that. Holly tried to get us to talk one day, but we both sat silently, not looking at each other, until she gave up and left the room.

Around this time, Rachel had married and was pregnant with her first child. She and I had lunch one day—I know it was in late June, the week after Father's Day. She didn't beat around the bush.

"I want to talk to you about Sammy."

I took a deep breath. "I'd rather not, honey."

"If not now, when?"

"Just not now, honey. It's too hard."

"I know." She reached across and put her hand over my folded hands. "But you have to fix it."

"Why is he doing this? Why won't he play baseball? Why won't he talk to me?"

"He doesn't want to play baseball. Or, he doesn't want to be forced to play baseball."

"I'm not forcing him."

Rachel sat back. "Really? What would you call it?"

"He could have been the starting shortstop this year."

"Dad. What if he doesn't care about that?"

"I don't understand."

"He's fifteen. Rebellious. Don't you remember how it was?" Rachel asked.

"No. I wasn't like that."

"But you didn't have a father at home to rebel against."

"He didn't even give me a Father's Day card."

"He's hurt and angry. He doesn't think you love him."

"That's not true!"

"Wait a minute now. I know you love him, and you know it, but he doesn't think so."

We sat quietly for a few minutes.

Rachel broke the silence. "I think I'm past the morning sickness."

"That's great, honey. Are you excited?"

"I'm starting to be. I hate being sick."

We were quiet again, but Rachel soon spoke. "Dad, I want to say one more thing about you and Sammy. You are the adult, so it's up to you. And don't wait too long. I'll bet Sammy is miserable."

I started to argue but held my tongue.

I looked across the table. Rachel was in tears. "It's too sad to see you two estranged." She reached down for the paper napkin to blot her eyes.

It took me a couple of more weeks to approach Sam Jr. I kept thinking about where and when to approach him and rehearsing what I would say. Finally, I came home from work one day, went right to his bedroom door, and knocked. There was no answer right away. I started to go into his room anyway but, instead, knocked again.

Finally, he called. "It's unlocked."

I entered, an angry feeling rising in me. But I pushed it down and said, "I'd like to talk. Can I sit down?"

"Sure." He had been lying back in the bed but sat up as I sat in the chair across from him in the corner of the room.

"I'm sorry for my yelling. You don't have to play baseball."

He didn't speak right away.

"I just thought you could've had a great year. Your fielding had really improved."

"Dad…" He didn't say more.

I decided to be quiet.

"I just want more free time. And I really don't like the new infield coach. He's super critical. I think I'm going to take up running. I can fit that in when it's convenient."

"Do you want me to talk to the coach?"

"No, Dad. Please don't do that. I'd rather not play."

"Okay. How's everything else? Your schoolwork? Is that girl who was here the other day your girlfriend?"

Sam Jr. smiled. "School's fine, and so's my girlfriend."

"What's her name?"

"Emily. She's in my English-literature class. She wants to be a poet."

"Great." I wanted to tell him I loved him, but it wouldn't come out. Instead, I asked, "Do you need any help with anything?"

"No, thanks, Dad. I'll let you know, though."

That was the end of our estrangement, but it took a while for things to warm up. Sam began to talk to me more, and he asked me to teach him about shad fishing the next spring. By the time he graduated from high school, we were close. And I figured out how to tell him I loved him.

Sam Jr. played basketball the next two years and was terrific as the team's point guard. He wasn't a big scorer, only averaged about nine points a game, but he was a great playmaker, averaged more than five assists, and knew how to control the pace of the game. He had a knack for when to speed it up and when to slow it down.

Sam did great in college. He didn't play varsity sports, but they had a well-organized intramural system there at Lehigh. I think his team won the intramural basketball championship his last two years. He majored in accounting, which I could never get my head around, but it obviously served him well. It was clear to me when he was a kid that he was determined about some things, and it solidified while he was at Lehigh. He was born with Holly's ambition.

I wish I saw more of Sam nowadays, but he has a demanding job in finance in New York, a wife, and two kids. I don't really understand what his job is, but I know he's doing well by his large home in North Jersey, the expensive SUVs in his three-car garage, and costly vacations they take. I hope he can keep whatever he has goin', goin'.

Holly and I drive over there quite a bit, but half the time, Sam's not there. He's traveling or working and likes to play golf. I'm an embarrassment on the golf course.

I'm happily retired, have five grandchildren, and stay busy even though I don't hunt or hike anymore. I stay in shape by working out several times a week at the Y. I keep my hand in the wrestling scene. I'm not head wrestling coach of the high school anymore, but I help in season. I have a consultant's contract with Penn State's wrestling program scouting high-school talent for them all over northeastern Pennsylvania. They usually give a couple of wrestling scholarships a year to the best wrestlers in our area, and I tell them who I think are the best. Some years they are only interested in a couple of weight classes because they already have plenty of talent in the other weight classes. A few years ago, they gave me a video camera, so nowadays I send them videos of the best candidates.

I spend a lot of time with Rachel's kids. She and her husband have a restaurant, and they're planning to open another one, so they're real busy. Frank, their oldest, is a high-school junior now and has his own car, so I don't drive him around anymore. But the other two need to go here or there to do this or that when their parents are busy at the restaurant. I love being their driver. They're kids, but they're good kids. The ten-year-old, Josie, is a pistol. She's always moving and fearless, so I have to keep an eye on her. She has trouble in school; they say she is "borderline ADHD," whatever the hell that is. I think it means she's delightful. Sometimes she jumps on me and hangs around my neck. I love it. Danny's six and just as sweet and calm as his sister is wild.

I joke that sometimes I have to make an appointment to spend time with my wife, and really, that is not too far from the truth. Holly has become an authority on environmental law. She doesn't have a full-time job, but I swear she works at least forty hours a week. And a lot of it involves travel, thankfully not across the country; it's usually to New York, Philly, or Washington DC. About six months ago, she testified in front of some environmental committee of Congress. I watched her on C-SPAN but didn't follow half of what she told them.

I hope she'll cut back soon, though. I can tell it's wearing her down, and I know she wants to spend more time with our grandchildren. She promised me that she would cut back too. If Holly makes a promise, you can take it to the bank. I hope it's soon.

Holly

I've only recently become reflective—a sign of age, I guess. I wouldn't say this out loud, but I'm proud of my accomplishments. I'm still surprised sometimes when professional people ask me for my opinion, but I've earned that respect. I've even learned to resist giving my advice until I'm asked. As I got into the middle stage of my legal career, I got aggressive and not at all reluctant to voice my opinions, sometimes loudly. Mr. Farlow, God bless him, came to the rescue again. He called me into his office one day for a conference call with an executive lawyer at one of the major oil companies.

We knew that the oil company did not want this case to go to trial, and our client hoped to avoid court as well. I had been negotiating with this guy off and on for months and could not reach a compromise.

Mr. Farlow and I and a stenographer sat around his conference table armed with legal pads and stacks of notes. We called, and Clyde, the lead lawyer for the oil company, answered on the first ring; we were expected.

"Clyde, this is Ted Farlow with Holly Kopco. How are you today?"

"I'm doing okay, Ted." Clyde's voice was guarded.

"You know we're calling about the McClure case."

"Right."

"Holly and I were talking earlier. We would like to close this case, and she thinks we may not be that far apart."

"That's not the way I see it. Her position is absurd."

"I have the file in front of me. Do you have a few minutes now to talk? Or, might you want to review things before?"

"I don't need the file; I have all the details in my head by now."

"Good. Let's see if we can resolve matters."

Mr. Farlow then proceeded to draw Clyde into a discussion of the case's details. He encouraged Clyde to express his perspective and did not challenge anything he said. In fact, he said things like "I see your point" or "We're not far apart there."

After fifteen minutes or so, Mr. Farlow said, "I think we can resolve things right now."

Clyde responded, "That's not the way I see it."

Then Mr. Farlow laid out a detailed proposal. It included two conditions that we knew were unacceptable to Clyde.

Clyde responded, saying, "I've already told Holly we can't do a lump-sum payment this fiscal year, and we won't pay eight percent interest for delayed payment of damages. And the mental-anguish claim is bogus."

Ted and I had already agreed among ourselves that we'd accept a delay in full payment and that we'd be flexible on the interest percentage.

Clyde continued. "Your client should bear half of the cleanup costs too."

"Okay, Clyde," Mr. Farlow continued. "How about I do this? I'll put a modified proposal together in writing and send it to you."

Within the month we settled the case, under almost the same terms that I had offered to Clyde earlier. When it was wrapped up, Mr. Farlow and I did a postmortem.

"Why do you think I got Clyde to agree to almost the same terms that you had offered?"

"I don't know. You were nicer to him than I was. He had gotten really hostile with me."

"You're on the right track. I think there were two things going on between Clyde and you. They were more *his* problem than yours, but you can learn something. He let his male ego cloud his judgment; it was a problem for him that you were a woman."

"I never tried any female tricks with him."

"I know, Holly. You didn't have to. I know Clyde—run into him at the club frequently. Women are fine as secretaries and legal assistants but not as full-fledged attorneys. He couldn't see your negotiations as lawyer to lawyer. He couldn't make real concessions to a woman."

I was quiet, reflecting about my negotiation with Clyde.

Mr. Farlow went on. "You're a terrific lawyer, Holly, and a good negotiator. But let me give you some advice about how to become a better negotiator."

I was all ears now. Mr. Farlow rarely gave specific feedback; that was one of the things I most liked about him. He let me discover things for myself.

"Learn to leave your ego somewhere else when you're negotiating. If the person across the table is hostile, try to put it aside. It's usually not personal. Focus on two things: your goals and the other guy's point of view. Get the person on the other side of the table to talk as much as you can and listen carefully to what he or she says. People often give you hints about what they want or how they think that are useful. And, if you're dealing with a man, be alert for suggestions that he might be letting your gender get in the way. I don't know what to suggest you do if you're dealing with a sex-biased man; you'll have to figure that out yourself."

Mr. Farlow looked a little embarrassed at that point. It made me smile. "Bingo," I said. "I don't know either, but I'll bet I can figure it out."

Mr. Farlow smiled then too. "I'll bet you do too," he said.

It took a while, but I did become a better negotiator. The big secret for me was focusing on the other person's point of view. I talked less and listened more. It was a big adjustment to tamp down my aggressiveness when I sensed the guy on the other side was having a problem dealing with a woman on equal terms. One time I realized that the guy I was dealing with was such a chest-thumping Neanderthal that he could not compromise with a woman. So I had one of our young guys call to close the deal.

I discovered another tactic that was helpful. When I sensed a conversation was getting to the head-butting stage, I backed off. Did what Mr. Farlow had done with the oil company guy: suggested that I send a written proposal. That created the space for the intensity to defuse, focused attention on the concrete details of the case, and eased settlement.

About two years after the negotiating conversation with Mr. Farlow, he died, had a massive heart attack in the locker room at the golf course right after he'd played eighteen holes. I was devastated, could not be consoled; it took me months to get over it. Still today, I get teary when I think of him. There is so much I never said to him, never thanked him enough for what he did for me. I was sad when my father died, but he was sick for a while before he passed on. It was sad, but he knew I loved him. I think the suddenness of Mr. Farlow's passing away increased the shock and grief I felt. I hope he understood how grateful I am.

I'm having trouble cutting back on work, have this dumb idea that I'm indispensable. But I want to move into more of a consulting role with the firm, and I've promised Sam that I'll cut back. I have a plan.

For a long time, Sam has wanted to take a trip across the country in a motor home. I don't want to travel with one of those huge "motels on wheels." I think it would feel like a bus trip. But I would like to take a long trip, and I think I can get Sam to agree to a trip where we'd stay in motels or hotels. We can afford it. If I get out of town for a long period and don't stay tethered to the firm by telephone, I can cut the cord—just check in once a week or so. I'm going to start planning with Sam this weekend.

Loretta

Nowadays, a half century after the Army Corps of Engineers gave up its Tocks Island Dam plan, I live quietly. Every so often, the local paper will print a story about the Tocks years, and I am brought back, but most days I'm happy with reading, working my garden, and church activities. I keep the books for my church, but since I've learned how to use computer software, it doesn't take much time. My grandchildren are grown now, so there's not much to do for them. I'm happy to observe them build their own lives, and they are kind to keep me involved.

I'm grateful for the Tocks Island Dam years. I feel satisfaction that I helped head off something that would have changed the Minisink Valley in ways most of us would have found objectionable. Instead, we got the Delaware Water Gap National Recreation Area. The natural character of our beloved Minisink was preserved. This has brought more people to the area, but they tend to be hikers and folks who value the natural character of the environment—a win-win, as they say.

Since Paul passed away, I'm sometimes lonely, especially in the morning and evening. I used to complain about Paul's morning energy. He'd wake up ready to go; seemed to go from deep sleep to hyperactive in an instant. He'd start talking right away, while my brain was still waking up. I must rely on the birds to help me wake up nowadays, and they're not reliable. I'd love to have Paul's morning chatter back.

In our later years together, Paul and I didn't go out much at night. We'd spend a couple of hours together in the living room, the television on but with the sound muted half the time. One of us might read. We didn't talk a lot, but this time was pleasurable for me. I don't spend much in the living room anymore. I often sit at the kitchen table to read; the light is better in there. If I do watch TV, it's usually in the bedroom. And I still watch with the sound off a lot of the time. Thank God, I'm a good sleeper, but I'll never get used to sleeping in that big bed by myself.

I notice conflicts like the Tocks Island Dam controversy still happen around the country. Most often nowadays, they seem to happen in the western United States, although they may not involve land grabs like Tocks did. For example, one that I followed last year was an oil pipeline running for miles on private land. Sometimes the little guy wins but more often not. We were lucky with Tocks. I'll bet if it hadn't been for Vietnam, the dam would've been built and God knows what it would be like around here now.

Last year, Monroe County gave me an award for the work I've done over the years. There were speeches by several politicians pointing to my work against the Tocks Island Dam and some later projects. Most people in the area are hardly aware of those tumultuous years, but there are enough old-timers still around to remind us. Holly Kopco gave a wonderful speech. She praised me a lot—called me a "Minisink Valley Treasure." That was wonderful, but she went on to talk passionately about environmental protection. It was impressive. The audience was impressed too; I could tell by watching their faces as she spoke. Holly has become quite a force.

As part of the award, they gave me a Waterford crystal vase. It sits on the mantle in the living room. It's beautiful, but I've been thinking lately that it's wasted in my living room, so I'm planning to give it to my daughter. But the last couple of times I saw her, I forgot to tell her to take it.

I'm beginning to fail. I fall sleep sitting up still holding a book, but I forget what I've read. My appetite is not good; food seems boring. Six months or so ago, I got scared about dying—mostly about what might precede actual death. I prayed about it and am peace with it most of the time. I still have moments, but they don't last. It's been a full life, but I do hope I go quickly and quietly in my own bed at home.

Will Mead

The Cloud Farm years are still vivid for me, and, thankfully, most of the sharp edges have rounded. There are plenty of positive memories. Times of struggle were mixed with periods of exhilaration and contentment. The four or five winter months between November and March were difficult every year. We had to work hard to stay warm and feed ourselves, often without electricity. I have clear images of us sitting at our kitchen table or in our living room wearing coats, hats, and gloves, our frosty breath hanging in the air. But I have cozy winter memories too. I recall one scene. About twenty of us, adults and children, were sitting and lounging in our living room, coatless for once, a fire crackling in the fireplace. Joe Caroline, who wrote fiction and poetry, was reading a short story he'd just finished. The electricity was off, so Joe's girlfriend, I think her name was Sara, was holding a flashlight over the dog-eared pages of the manuscript he held.

I've forgotten the details of Joe's story, but the setting and mood are vivid to me. Our son Kurt was asleep in Rosemary's arms, and everyone one else, adults and children, were listening closely. I was engrossed by the scene, by the collective contentment I saw, the state of mind I'd imagined would result from living in a successful, peaceful collective community. I was reassured that night that our enterprise was worth the effort.

Today my daughter, Diana, has good memories of those years in the Minisink Valley. And the influence of those years on her are still visible; she dresses like a twenty-first-century hippie. But all the lessons didn't take: she's firmly grounded in American capitalism, the head of an independent publisher of children's literature. Kurt was still an infant when we left and has no memory of Cloud Farm. I wish Rosemary was still around to see Diana's success, but she passed away a few years ago after discovering a melanoma on her back too late for successful treatment.

It's easy, four decades later, to understand we were naïve to think we could establish a viable permanent community in those circumstances. Government was not going to tolerate us living rent-free on public land for the long term. Local people associated us with the Tocks Island Dam, and their hostility grew steadily over time. As our numbers increased, many newcomers were not committed to our ideals. They enjoyed living free of social conventions, especially our tolerance of marijuana use and permissive sex mores, but they were unwilling to engage in the hard work required for economic viability.

Finally, winter in the Pocono Mountains is harsh. Most of us did not have working central-heating systems in our houses, and some had no running water. The hardships eroded our ideals and gradually, under pressure from law enforcement, extinguished our commitment. But the story of our successes and struggles is an interesting one.

The problems I refer to here were not so visible when we were in the throes of trying to build our community. Looking back, I can see how my zeal for making things work, blinded me to the realities of our situation. But from a distance, it's also true that those years at Cloud Farm were some of the best of my life; Rosemary and I were happiest there after I gave up my extracurricular sex. Some interesting and creative people lived in our community. Most of us were fully engaged by what we were doing. We were physically strong and vigorous. I'm about twenty pounds heavier now, but those ideals, well, ideals have a way of sticking around.

I still have a local friend from the Cloud Farm years—Sam Kopco. Ours is an unlikely friendship. Sam grew up in the Minisink, was a lineman for the power company, liked to hunt, and was a combat Vietnam veteran. He's a smart guy but not formally educated. I'm city bred, with sixteen years of formal education, was opposed to the Vietnam War, and feel bad when I step on a spider. Sam and I enjoyed sharing a joint from time to time; I had a reliable connection for high-quality pot in New York City. Pot helped smooth our differences.

My father had a term to describe men he admired. "He's a class guy," he would say. For a long time, I didn't understand what it was about a man who earned my father's "class guy" designation. It confused me because some such men lacked physicality. You could get the class-guy designation more easily if you were physically impressive, but I noted that a few of my father's class guys were not like that. Our undersized neighborhood butcher was a class guy, as was a mild-mannered parish priest, an occasional politician, and my maternal grandfather who was a bookkeeper. One was a Quaker.

One day in my early twenties, I asked my father to explain what it meant to be a class guy. His responses resulted in the longest conversation I ever had with him. He told me stories; stories about men he knew that illustrated his class-guy criteria. He didn't talk explicitly about morals or courage or charity or other such concepts. But the stories illustrated these principles.

Years after our conversation, I defined for myself what these principles are. To get the class-guy attribution from my father, a man had to live by a moral code, not necessarily grounded in religion; had to be a dependable and loyal friend; and—this surprised me—a class guy had to be kind. He could not be a bully or a braggart.

Sam Kopco is at the top of my class-guy list.

A few months ago, Sam and I got together for dinner in New York City, and he stayed with me overnight. We don't get together very often, and when we do, it's usually only for a few hours. But this time, his wife, Holly, was in Washington overnight on business. Neither one of us smokes pot anymore, but we were sipping my favorite sour mash bourbon in my small living room. I sold my house and live in a modest-size condo in Brooklyn.

We were watching the 10:00 p.m. news. One after another, short segment about trouble here and there: budget fights in Congress, murders in Chicago, a public-transportation-worker strike somewhere else, a suicide bombing in Pakistan, a terrorist attack in France, and a famine in Sudan. But recently, public conflict in New York City had ebbed, and the city seemed to be functioning well. I had the sound muted during a commercial break.

Sam spoke. "Do things seem as fucked up in the country as they were when we were young?"

"I wonder about that too, Sam. It's different today. It seems there's more violence and disorder in the world than back in the sixties and seventies. But then I think about the assassinations and riots back then and realize that we're a lot better informed. With all the cable channels and other media, we get news we never heard about fifty years ago."

Sam took this in. "I think there's more war. Vietnam was bad and went on too long. But we've had wars going on all over Africa and the Middle East for years. They're not as big as Vietnam, but there's more of them."

"When the Cold War ended, when the Soviet Union collapsed, I thought we might have a long, peaceful time. It didn't last very long," I said.

Sam changed the subject. "Our young people seem different to me."

"How so?"

"They seem more serious. Most of them have a plan for after high school. They're not as respectful manners wise, but they're not disrespectful either. It's hard to put into words."

"How about your wrestlers? Are they different from when you were wrestling?"

"Yeah, they are. They're in better condition physically and have a better grip on techniques. Don't seem as determined, though. I used to think they weren't as tough, but I don't think that's it. Maybe it's to do with team. It's more an individual thing nowadays."

"That's interesting. As a sociologist, I'd say what you're describing is the individual being more important than the group."

"Maybe that's it. Team was more important back then."

"Are the *times* more tumultuous?"

"I don't know about that," Sam answered. "Things seemed pretty crazy to me."

"It's really hard to draw a comparison. Back then I wanted to be part of a social and political revolution, so the disarray seemed a good thing to me—what we were trying to make happen. I understand it was very different for you, though."

"Yeah. For a couple of years, I was having trouble holding things together. After I recovered physically, I looked around, and it seemed like everything would unravel around me. It's good I came back to the Minisink. Eventually, I knew I could count on the community to hold me up."

"And you found Holly."

"Oh yeah. That was crucial."

"But are you saying the country seems fucked up again?"

"Right. The country itself is messed up."

"This is a lot of dysfunction, I agree."

The weather report had come onto the TV, so I unmuted the volume to listen.

I turned the television off after the weather report.

"I hope I live long enough to see what happens," Sam mused.

"I'm going to have another bourbon. Can I pour you one?"

"I've been waiting for you to ask. I think we've solved all the world's problems."

When we finished those bourbons, we were ready for bed.

Jack Neumann

I hadn't been back to the Minisink Valley in almost forty years. In fact, I avoid thinking about the Tocks Island Dam years at all. I've understood for a long time that the failure to build the dam had little to do with my performance. The design engineers, the politicians, the emerging environmental movement, and the lack of funding all share the blame. But I still feel a vague sense of failure, and, unfortunately, the Army Corps of Engineers bureaucracy, unable to assign blame elsewhere, held me, the project director, accountable. Naïvely back then, I thought I'd be able to move on in the Corps without prejudice. Big delusion.

After Tocks failed, my next assignment was to manage a small sewer-installation project in Wyoming—a $1 or $2 million job that took only a few months to complete. The Tocks Island Dam project's cost was more than $100 million and would have taken years to complete. Initially, I hoped that my assignment in Wyoming would be a one-time punishment, but when I was given another low-cost, short-term assignment, I saw the handwriting on the wall and left the Corps.

By most measures, my subsequent career was a huge success. I went to work for a modest-size construction outfit in Northern California that grew fast, and in only a few years, I was a principal in the company, making a high salary and big bonuses. My family and I came to love living in Northern California, and we have retired there with no plans to leave.

Our children are raised. After college, my son went into the corporate side of the movie business in Los Angeles and is doing well. My daughter, Mary, came back to the east coast and now manages a nonprofit in Philadelphia. My son has three children, and my daughter has two.

My father passed away in 2002. Fortunately, he was only sick and disabled for three or four months before he died. He stayed active until late 2001, had even gone to the 9/11 disaster site in Lower Manhattan to help. My mother turned ninety-six this year and has finally agreed to move into assisted living at a nice facility in Bucks County, Pennsylvania. This is what brought me back to the Minisink Valley.

We had a family reunion in the Poconos before Mom moved into assisted living. There were twelve of us—my wife and I, Mom, my son and his family, and my daughter and her family. We rented two three-bedroom houses for a week, just four miles above the Delaware Water Gap. I was nervous about going back to the area, hesitant about being reminded of the failed dam project I directed there so long ago.

I had a great time and shed the Tocks demon. The morning after we moved into our rented homes, I drove alone to Stroudsburg and then up River Road past some of the land we had condemned for the Tocks Island Dam. Nothing was familiar. I knew the location where we had mistakenly demolished an old church. It was heavily wooded and looked as if it had been undisturbed for a generation. It occurred to me that it had been two generations since we'd desecrated the place.

I drove further north and parked at a spot overlooking the Delaware River. There was a young family with three children eating at a picnic table about a hundred feet from where I parked. The youngest child was still in diapers and kept scurrying away from the family toward the steep trail down to the river. Every two minutes one of the parents or the oldest child, an eight- or nine-year-old girl, would chase after him. They finally strapped him into a mobile high chair at the end of the picnic table, and he expressed his displeasure loudly—not by crying, no; instead, he screamed as if he was being tortured. The father finally took him out of his chair and followed as he headed straight down the path to the river. I watched until the two of them dropped below my field of vision.

There were canoes on the river. Every minute, two or three would pass by, most with a pair of paddlers. They were almost all red—the canoes, that is—and, I assumed, rented from the same place. The view was noiseless, except for the chatter of the family at the picnic table. The father and toddler had returned from their visit to the river. The child was eating whatever was on the tray of his high chair as quickly as he could get it in his mouth.

It was a wonderful week. We rented canoes one day and spent hours on the river, did some hiking, went to eat at a restaurant twice but mostly stayed together and read, napped, and played cards and board games. My mother was happy that week. Every time I looked at her, there was a quiet smile on her face. There was a hint of sadness among us. Even the children seemed to understand their grandmother's life was about to change and that the passage was a sad one.

I never saw my mother again. She died in her sleep two months after entering assisted living. Somehow, my mother's life and death, and the failed Tocks Island Dam have merged for me, left me a slight sense of sadness about it all.

Sam and Holly

We went to Loretta Shuster's funeral in October 2017. Both of us were struck by the failure in her final accolades to recognize her role in preserving the natural state of the Minisink Valley. The preacher didn't even mention her founding of Lower Minisink Environmental Defense. We spoke to her daughter after the service; even she didn't seem to seem to appreciate the essential role her mother played in stopping the construction of the Tocks Island Dam.

There was a luncheon at the Mountain Inn after the funeral service. We counted thirty-eight people in attendance. We estimated that more than half of the attendees were born after the collapse of the dam project or were too young at the time to understand its importance. We could identify only two people who we were sure knew about Loretta's role in the preservation of the Minisink. One was the woman who had enforced the exclusion of Holly's from the county's land records. Her name was Liz, but neither of us could recall her last name. The other was a banker from our local credit union. We thought his name was Sid.

During lunch, we had a sense that the value of Loretta's life had been overlooked. During dessert, Holly went to the podium and microphone that had been used only for a few welcoming remarks by Loretta's son and the preacher's premeal invocation.

"Excuse me. I hope you don't mind if I interrupt dessert for a few moments to say something about my friend Loretta Shuster."

The room quieted.

"I'm Holly Kopco. Most of you don't know me, but many of you remember my husband, Sam, over there."

Holly pointed to me at a table on her right.

"Sam was the high-school wrestling coach for many years."

Someone shouted, "Go, Sam."

Holly continued, "It's a long time ago now—almost forty years, when Loretta saved the Minisink Valley."

The room quieted further. Folks who had been concentrating on their peach cobbler put down their forks. Others who were sitting with their backs toward Holly turned to face her.

"For almost a decade in the 1960s and 1970s, the federal government and some local interests were intent on building a dam across the Delaware River several miles above the Water Gap. The dam would have interrupted the natural flow of the Delaware River and created a huge lake in place of it. In preparation for construction of the dam, the federal government forced hundreds of families to sell their homes and farms. Most of those people have passed on, but I'll wager that some of you here today have grandparents or other relatives who were among the displaced. It is not an exaggeration to say that livelihoods were devastated and lives were lost as a result."

I could tell that Holly was beginning to feel the emotion of her words. She leaned forward, grasped the sides of the rostrum, and went on to describe the trouble experienced by several families that had lost their land—including the suicide of Vera Lutz. The room was silent now.

"Excavation of the damsite was about to begin, but it had become known that there was a geological fault under the damsite, and other negative environmental consequences would result if the dam was built. There were strong forces in local, state, and federal government, and among those who would profit from increased tourism, though, and those who opposed the dam were not organized."

Holly paused and looked around the room, seeming to make eye contact with everyone. Then, in a deeper voice, she said, "Do you know who was the strongest force in opposition to the dam? Who effectively and successfully organized the opposition? Loretta Shuster."

I looked over and saw Loretta's daughter blotting her eyes with a tissue.

Holly spoke for another few minutes discussing the role of the Lower Minisink Environmental Defense, relating an anecdote or two. She concluded by saying, "Thank you for listening. I hope I haven't violated any boundaries. But I wanted all of you to know how Loretta helped preserve our beautiful valley. She is one of my heroes. She was a mentor to me as well. I haven't known anyone else in my life whose strength of character was wrapped in such a soft cloak of humility."

Loretta's daughter stopped Holly on her way back to our table; I watched the two of them hold each other. And me, I was again impressed and proud of my Holly. She never fails to step up when something needs to be done.

It turned out that a retired reporter for our local newspaper was in the audience to hear Holly's tribute to Loretta Shuster. He called Holly at home later that evening. His newspaper had published Loretta's obituary the day after she died, but it paid only passing attention to her role as the founder of the environmental defense group. The reporter wrote a much more expansive obituary for Loretta that got a lot of attention.

Stroudsburg recognized Loretta's contribution a few months later. There was a ceremony at the courthouse, and a plaque was mounted on the wall just inside the doors at the main entrance. They also began a Loretta Shuster Memorial Award with a $500 prize for the local high-school student who wrote the best essay about environment protections for the Minisink Valley. Loretta's great-granddaughter won the first scholarship.

LAD
ML   MAR   2018

Made in the USA
Lexington, KY
17 February 2018